CAROLYN R. SCHEIDIES

A Proper Guardian

HEARTSONG
PRESENTS

Recycling programs
for this product may
not exist in your area.

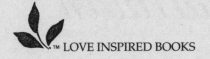

™ LOVE INSPIRED BOOKS

ISBN-13: 978-0-373-48668-7

A PROPER GUARDIAN

Copyright © 2013 by Carolyn R. Scheidies

www.LoveInspiredBooks.com

Printed in U.S.A.

Delight thyself also in the Lord,
and he shall give thee the desires of thine heart.
—*Psalms* 37:4

Life is never simple or straightforward.
There are lots of dips, discouragements and long
stretches of drought along with the bursts of wonder,
satisfaction and unexpected joys. My novel writing
parallels life. I began my foray into book publication
at Heartsong when they started the line at
Barbour Publishing. I am gratified to come
full circle, writing for Heartsong again now that it
is with Harlequin. I am thankful for all those who
believed in me along the way, even when I haven't
believed in myself—friends, family, agent and editors.

Chapter 1

1803

Winter bowed her head over the ornamented desk. "Lord, I'm so tired and lonely. Why did You have to take father away?" With a sigh, she ran her small, crooked fingers over the elegant scrollwork of the desk. Here she felt her father's presence as nowhere else. Here she diligently worked on the estate books as her father had done for so many years. Here, at this desk beside her father, she had learned to handle estate affairs.

By the time he passed away, the tenant farmers felt comfortable approaching her with their problems, considering her both honest and fair. But the responsibility of running the entire estate by herself had taken its toll on the fragile young woman. She straightened and stretched, trying to dissipate the stiffness in her muscles from the hours of work over the heavy books.

There was no one else, no son to inherit. The rolling fertile land, the long red-stone Renton Hall, the overseeing of staff and tenants, the duty hers and hers alone. The task wearied her even as it gave her purpose.

Winter pushed back her waist-length brunette hair, unaware of the silver highlights sparkling through it. She preferred having Mrs. Duncan pull her hair to the sides, leaving the rest streaming down her back. She tried to rub her stiff shoulder, but her inflexible fingers could only assuage the stiffness slightly.

She stretched her equally stiff leg, grimaced at the flash of pain through her thigh and knee and clenched her teeth. She wondered, not for the first time, what her life might have been if the arrogant cup-shot peer driving the high-perch phaeton had managed to avoid their carriage. What if their carriage had not overturned, breaking her mother's neck and crippling her?

Shaking her head to clear away the anger, she cried out, "Lord, why? Why did You take father, as well? I know he was ill, but…"

Slowly lowering her leg, Winter smoothed the skirts of the white-sashed, deep rose muslin gown that hugged her young maturing figure. Recalling the wide full skirts her mother always wore, Winter smiled at her simple practical gowns, designed to be comfortable with a minimum of underskirts and fullness.

Since she neither subscribed to fashion magazines nor mixed in society, she had no idea her practical gown reflected the new French simplicity in fashion. She only knew her gowns fit comfortably and swished gracefully around her feet.

Again she smoothed down the skirt, liking the feel of the soft material under her palm. "Papa, you don't mind I save black for what few guests I have, do you? I know you said we should not mourn excessively, but it's…it's only been four months. Oh, Papa."

She blinked her long dark lashes over expressive deep blue eyes that dominated her oval face. Despite her grief, she held a maturity belying her small stature and delicate bone structure.

Laying down her pen, Winter rubbed her sore wrist. Even without a scold from the family butler, Richard Duncan, she knew she needed a break.

Jupiter, her iron-gray gelding, would be only too eager for a hard ride up Renton Hill. Then there was dear Mutton-head. Winter smiled. The little black puppy had been her father's last gift. Exasperated at their unsuccessful attempts to train the wriggly puppy, he called him Mutton-head and the name stuck.

Thanks to her father's prudent management, life here was good, if lonely. How she wished for someone in whom she could confide her fears and share the burden of dealing with the estate. With disgust, Winter thought of her nearest neighbors.

Hardly had her father been buried before Lord Nelson stopped in. Portly and pompous, he started by offering condolences. In the next breath he said, "Ah, my dear. With no one to inherit, you are now alone. Surely a wee thing like yourself will not be staying on."

"I…"

He gave her no time to answer as he plowed on. "As your father's dear friend…"

She grimaced at this fabrication, but still he took no notice. "I am here to make an offer. Generous, of course. Will give you enough to find a chaperone and establish yourself in London."

"Lord Nelson. Lord Nelson. *My lord,*" she yelled to get his attention, thinking he must certainly be partially deaf. "I am staying right here."

Lord Nelson stepped back in surprise. "But my dear. This is not seemly. Not seemly at all."

With a plastered-on smile she had Duncan show him the door.

His behavior showed at least a modicum of concern. Anthony's approach had been quite odd, to say the least, considering their less-then-amicable relationship. Then again,

Winter admitted, Viscount Derik's behavior had never born much scrutiny.

A few days after Lord Nelson's visit, Anthony, dressed in what Winter imagined was the first style of elegance, sauntered into her parlour for all the world as though he already owned Renton Hall.

Bowing low over her hand, he held it so long she snatched it away, knowing from the chill of his palm how much he shrank from her touch. Frowning, he said, "I do not wish for you to be alone at this terrible time of grief. I don't want you to be alone now or in the future." He cleared his throat, hesitated as though considering carefully, "Winter, I am asking for your hand."

She gaped at him in astonishment. An arrogant smile touched the corners of his thin lips.

In her vulnerability, she took his proposal seriously. She glanced up at the rather hard features framed by dark curly hair, took in his lean muscular body. She could do worse. "I do not understand this. You can not possibly have feelings for me, and I have never much cared for you, Lord Derik. Mayhap with time…"

Leaning back, the viscount shook his head, "My dear Winter. Time we don't have."

"I don't love you, Anthony." Winter clasped her hands. She hated being in this position.

Lord Derik tucked a tendril of hair behind her ear, making her shiver. "Winter, love has very little to do with my offer."

At her confusion, Anthony wrapped an arm around her shoulders. "Winter, don't get in a taking over my words. They are, after all, only true. Your father is gone now. You are alone here, and this is for your protection."

Winter moved away from his embrace. "Anthony, I…"

Hurriedly he continued, "We've known each other forever and our estates march side by side. Combining our estates would make us one of the largest landowners between here and London. Think about it. Marry me and you spend the rest of your life in comfort. No longer would you need concern yourself with ledgers, finances and disgruntled farmers."

It almost sounded good. "I don't know." She stared into Lord Derik's eyes. There was something in his gaze that gave her pause, though she could not put a name to her fear. She got to her feet.

He seemed to sense her thoughts and frowned. "What is there to consider?" He tried to pull her down beside him again. When she moved away, he also stood and stared down on her. "Your bloodlines are impeccable, Winter. Surely you want children."

The flicker in her eyes made him press his suit. "You'll make a good mother, Winter. What more do you want?"

"I am not a brood mare up for sale, Anthony."

She could tell he kept his temper under control with difficulty. Lord Derik took her arm. "Listen, Winter. We'll get along just fine. I'll treat you well. You have my word on that. Besides, you go your way, and I'll go mine."

Winter whispered, "What of love?"

"This is the nineteenth century. We're not peasants to marry for some fleeting passion. We're above all that. Marriage is for the merging of property and bloodlines. To put it bluntly—to beget an heir." He paused, releasing Winter's arm.

"After you produce an heir, you can, discreetly, of course, find someone to love you. Surely you don't expect me to be faithful. I'm sorry, Winter, but…" He shrugged and spoke almost with regret. "I won't be. I'm not the faithful sort."

Her eyes widened at this blatant admission. "Viscount Derik, unless a man loves me, I will not marry him. Father left Renton Estates to me, and I will manage just fine."

"Who else would have you?" His words, though quietly spoken, stabbed her heart.

Blinking back tears, she tugged the bell cord. To her relief, Duncan answered almost immediately.

"My lady?"

"Please show the Viscount out." With a curt nod, Winter watched Anthony, his shoulders stiff and tense, march toward the door.

Turning, he managed a smile. "At least I'm honest, Winter. Think about my offer."

The door closed, and she was alone. Wrapping her arms about herself, Winter tried to still her shivering. "Lord, somehow he frightens me. You know how cruel he has sometimes been in the past. He has a large estate. He doesn't need mine. Does he want power, Lord? Is this about greed or is there something else?"

No answer came. Anthony's words returned. Hurtful though they were, Winter knew them for the truth. Who would want a woman with a disability such as hers? Deep inside, a part of her cried, while another part picked up the pieces and prepared to go on.

A smile pulled at the corners of her lips as a verse filled her mind from Hebrews 13. *I will never leave thee, nor forsake thee.*

"Thank You, Lord, for reminding me that even if I have no one else, You will provide for me."

Blake's poem "The Tiger" hummed in her mind. It was her favorite among the poems by William Blake. Softly she quoted the poem taught to her by her father after the accident that took the life of her mother.

For the first time, she wondered if the learning of the poem hadn't given him, and herself, the strength to go on.

Tiger, Tiger, burning bright
In the forests of the night,
What immortal hand or eye
Could frame thy fearful symmetry?

In what distant deeps or skies
Burnt the fire of thine eyes?

On what wings dare he aspire?
What the hand, dare seize the fire?

Somewhere inside Winter felt that strength. God would take care of her.

Tiger, Tiger, burning bright. The words continued to sound their refrain. Again she had been remembering rather than working. Not able to concentrate, Winter got up from the desk, letting her long full sleeves billow over her hands, and headed toward the door.

Before she made it halfway across the room, Duncan appeared in the doorway. "Oh, excuse me, my lady. I had no idea you were finished here."

For the first time, Winter noticed his graying hair and the slight stoop to his shoulders. For her, he would always be the smiling man who gave in to her whims when she was in leading strings.

"I thought I'd have Jupiter saddled and take a ride."

"Very good, miss. But I have someone here to see you." Before Winter could respond, he announced, "Justin Stuart, Earl of Alistair."

Tall and commanding, Lord Alistair strode into the room, dwarfing the small study by his presence. Winter closed her mouth with a snap as she took in the giant of a man who wore his well-tailored blue coat, lighter colored waistcoat and white breeches with casual indifference. Yet his manner kept Winter from classifying him as a dandy. More like, she thought as she surveyed the amusement in his gray eyes and the dark, wind-tossed hair, *a rake.*

Lord Alistair. She recalled the name, now, along with the rumors of his exploits in London. Her dark images of him did not match the solid strength that kept her from dismissing him out of hand.

Lord Alistair's eyes darkened as Winter surveyed him with

a snap of anger in her eyes. Her frankly disapproving appraisal seemed to disconcert him.

Winter sighed. *Lord,* she appealed silently, *do I have to contend with Lord Alistair, too?*

She could think of only two reasons he might be paying her a call and both infuriated her. "Well, what brings you to the door, a marriage of convenience to get your hands on the inheritance to squander on your vices, or an equally offensive offer for the estate?"

Lord Alistair took a step back and stared down at her as she glared up at him, daring him to speak. He brought himself up sharply. "Neither," he said in a deep, controlled voice. "I came on behalf of Lord Renton's daughter. I wish to speak with her."

Winter's eyebrows lifted. So his high-in-the-instep lordship had not made the connection. "Why, may I ask?"

Irritation crossed his face, and he examined her as though she was beneath his dignity. He probably thought of her as a little less than a glorified servant. Lord Alistair growled, "I have come to make provisions for the child. Now, miss, whatever your name is, as her nurse..."

Winter scarcely heard the last as she repeated. "Provisions? What provisions? Why does Lady Renton need the likes of someone like you?"

"Why, to see to her future care." Lord Alistair leaned against the nearby shelf as though he found it awkward to converse with an obstinate female.

Anxiety clouded Winter's eyes as she stifled a shiver of fear. "Please," she whispered, "tell me plainly of what you speak. Why should you have ought to do with my...ah, her care? Lord Renton died over four months ago. It seems rather odd for you to show up here now."

Guilt crossed Lord Alistair's face. He shifted as her inquiry appeared to hit home. "I can see you are not about to let me see the child until I clarify my position."

Pulling out the guardianship papers, he unfolded them and

flashed them in front of Winter. "You do read, don't you?" Sarcasm laced his tone.

At her nod, he added, "Lord Renton appointed me guardian of his daughter and trustee of his estate."

Winter rocked back in shock. "Fustian! How is that possible?"

Lord Alistair appeared to enjoy the effect his pronouncement had on her. Straightening, he took a menacing step toward her, deliberately, she sensed, to overpower her with his height. "You heard correctly. I want to see the girl, and I want to see her straightaway."

Instantly, Winter's astonishment turned to anger aimed both at her father and at this arrogant stranger trying to intimidate her. "No! How could he?" she blurted, clenching and unclenching her hands. "I've run this estate for almost two years. I do not require some meddlesome lord taking over."

Her tone bitter, she added, "What do you plan to do, lock Lady Renton away somewhere? Let her rot?"

Surprise flashed across Lord Alistair's expression. "No, I have no intention of removing the girl from her home. I do intend to ensure she and the estate are properly looked after."

After hesitating, he said, "If you fear for your job, mayhap we can work out some arrangement."

His piercing stare faded when Winter bit her lips to suppress her bubble of laughter. A puzzled frown crossed his lean features. "Does my boldness so amuse you then?"

Winter's anger faded into a choked laugh at the man's bold assessment. Actually, having never seen herself as a desirable woman, the situation struck her as funny. If only the arrogant lord realized. She tried to swallow the giggles. The odious man deserved her sharpest set-down.

But the confusion and pique on Lord Alistair's face was too much and a giggle escaped before she could recall it. "M'lord—" she forced herself to swallow another giggle "—I think we had better talk."

She nodded toward the door. "Please, I will meet you in the east parlour, down the hall to your left."

Lord Alistair hesitated. "And the girl?"

Another giggle escaped. "I, ah, promise you, you will meet Lady Renton."

Dismissed, Lord Alistair strode out of the room, his face flushing as the girl's laughter followed him down the dark-paneled hallway to the parlour. There he paced the room, waiting for the insolent young woman to bring Lord Renton's daughter to him. He wished himself anywhere but here.

For certain, the petite young woman with the long silky hair would need to learn how to deal with her betters if she planned on staying. Strangely, for all her insolence, he very much wished her to stay. He reviewed his own behavior with discomfort and found it wanting. Unlike most of his contemporaries, he prided himself in not seeking to seduce the vulnerable young women in the employ of the houses in which he was often a guest.

Annoyed as much with himself as with the young woman, Lord Alistair sat near the wide windows in a large graceful rose silk-covered arm chair. He noticed the matching chair opposite appeared somewhat higher than his own and wondered.

A fire in the grate of the huge black marble fireplace warmed the room, which held a chill in the early spring afternoon. Over the mantel hung a gilded framed Piranese.

Lord Alistair turned away. He much preferred the rich depth of Rembrandt.

"What's keeping the girl?" His brows dipped with irritation. A man used to commanding and intimidating others, Lord Alistair found himself waiting on a slip of a girl, a girl who laughed in his face. Then again, she did have to fetch Renton's daughter.

Sitting up, Lord Alistair began to wonder just how badly the girl was disabled.

Was she being taken advantage of by the young woman? Why had he not asked more questions of Lord Renton? Lord Alistair ran his hand through his hair, revealing his impatience and frustration. He stopped, a rueful grin on his face. His valet continually scolded him for a habit that destroyed the styling of his hair. Still, his thoughts disturbed him.

Not only did he not know the girl's condition, but he also did not even know her name or age.

"Why did I get myself into this?"

Chapter 2

Winter's giggles faded in her returning anger. Hands on her hips, she declared to no one in particular, "How dare the man think he can walk into my life after four months and take over."

With a jerk, she pulled the bell cord to summon Duncan.

"M'lady?"

"Please bring tea into the east parlour for his lordship and myself."

The aging butler touched his forehead respectfully. "As you wish, my lady." Winter saw the question in his eyes, but only nodded to him as he left to do her bidding.

A short while later he returned, pushing a narrow tea cart. He made no comment as Winter fell in behind him.

As she hoped, with his gaze on the butler, Lord Alistair missed her limping into the room in the butler's shadow.

As Duncan set up the tea service, Winter slipped into the chair opposite her unwanted visitor. Only when the manservant spoke did Lord Alistair notice her already sitting composed and assured in the other chair.

"Miss, do you wish to serve?" Duncan often lapsed in the more informal "miss." Winter merely smiled.

"Thank you, no. Please pour, Duncan." Picking up the delicate willow-patterned Bow china teapot with surprisingly gentle hands, the old manservant poured into the tiny china cups. Hot scones and fair-sized sandwiches filled an oblong china plate that Duncan offered Lord Alistair after handing round the tea.

"Don't be shy, m'lord, I am sure you are hungry after your long ride—from London I presume."

As the manservant quietly left the room, Lord Alistair met Winter's gaze with a frown. "Well, where is Lord Renton's daughter?" His frown deepened. "I am tired of your games, miss." He hesitated. How had the butler addressed her?

Amusement danced in Winter's eyes as she pushed up her sleeve and gracefully leaned forward to pick up her cup. Cradling the delicately painted teacup in her palm, Winter leaned back to take in the stunned look on Lord Alistair's face.

"I am Winter Joy Renton."

With satisfaction, she watched the dull red creep up his cheeks. Her large eyes challenged him. He met her challenge with a sheepish grin. "My most humble apologies, Lady Renton. I thought... Fustian, how was I to know?"

Winter felt the flush blossoming in her own cheeks. "I've never been considered in that light before."

"I truly am sorry, Lady Renton. I don't usually... Not innocent misses," he stammered, and Winter sensed he condemned himself.

He winced. "I don't consider myself in their number. You are lovely, you know. I meant that. But I had no right to make insinuations, and I beg your forgiveness."

Glancing up, she said, "You are forgiven, for that. However, this fustian about being my guardian." Her voice hardened. "Lord Alistair, I am not some simpering miss just out of the schoolroom, and I am fully capable of handling my own affairs."

"Your father did not trust your neighbors. He feared they would pressure you into one or another undesirable arrangement. From your first challenge when I arrived—" he smiled at her before continuing "—I believe you have been pressured."

Winter pushed back hair that fell over her shoulder. "How could father make such arrangements without even telling me?"

From his knowing expression, she knew he heard the plea in her voice. "Your father cared about you, Winter."

"Why you, of all people?" Winter asked. "Father strictly followed the teachings of Wesley, and you…" She shrugged.

"I am honest, whatever else I may be." Winter watched fire flash in Lord Alistair's eyes at her judgment and wondered. "When I was still in leading strings, Mother was converted in a Wesley revival. If that means anything to you."

"I understand she and my mother were bosom bows." Winter sipped her tea.

"Yes, and your father was sensible enough to know I would have no designs on either his estate or his daughter." Lord Alistair set his cup down on the table next to the chair.

Winter colored. "No one else does, either. The Viscount Derik merely wishes to merge property and bloodlines." She shrugged and turned away, but not, she realized, before Lord Alistair saw the pain reflected in her eyes.

She grimaced. "Anthony acts as though he does me a favor by accepting me as his wife."

Lord Alistair sucked in a deep breath. "His offer came as a shock then?"

Winter closed her eyes a moment before answering. "Anthony has never been overly concerned with my sensibilities."

"This might be the best offer of marriage you may ever receive, Winter."

Winter glared at him. "You, too!" She set her cup down with

a crash that almost shattered the delicate china. "I shall not marry anyone unless I love him with all my heart." Her voice rose. "I don't expect you to understand, but even if I never marry, I will not settle for anything less. Whatever Anthony has in mind, I do not love him that way."

"You are fortunate to have the choice, Winter. Most young women do not."

"I suppose now that you are my guardian you shall try to force me into some marriage of convenience to get me off your hands."

Lord Alistair glanced away. "I…" Winter's eyes flashed fire, drawing a refrain from Lord Alistair. "'Tiger, tiger, burning bright…'"

The words startled Winter. "You are familiar with *Songs of Experience* by Blake?"

"Indeed. One of my favorites." He smiled. "Your eyes are tiger's eyes when you become angry."

"I'm impressed." Maybe he wasn't such a coxcomb after all.

"I do read," he commented dryly.

"As for forcing me up the altar…" Winter's gaze narrowed.

"Let's leave all that for later, shall we? Right now, I'd like to look over your books."

Stifling her retort, Winter shrugged. "I suppose I have little choice."

Slowly, gracefully, she got to her feet. As Lord Alistair followed her, she felt his gaze on her bad leg. Tensing, Winter glanced up. "Are you coming?"

In the study, she motioned toward the sturdy desk chair and stepped back to let her new guardian sit down.

"The books are in here." She struggled to haul out a heavy ledger only to have Lord Alistair cover her hand with his own.

"Here, permit me."

His sensitivity to her stirred Winter strangely. "Thank you, Lord Alistair."

Lord Alistair stared straight into her eyes. "Justin, if you please."

"But as my guardian, Lord Alistair."

He traced her soft trembling lips with his gaze. "Justin. I am not some dotty old man."

At his coaxing smile, she relaxed. He was, after all, her guardian—however undesired. "As you wish, Justin."

"That wasn't so difficult was it?" He turned toward the book open in front of him, quickly scanning the clear, legible writing on page after page. Notes on each page detailed each entry. "I'm impressed," he said, not realizing Winter had already quietly slipped away.

In her room, she tore at the lacings of her gown. "Mrs. Duncan, quick. Help me into my riding habit."

The gray-haired woman brought Winter her black wool habit. "My Duncan says your father made Lord Alistair your guardian. Is it true?"

"Unfortunately so, Mrs. Duncan. Why didn't father tell me?" Winter asked as the old family retainer helped her into her riding skirt.

She was once again the lost young girl who, after losing her mother and her own health, turned for comfort to the matronly servant.

"I don't know, my lady, but I do know your father cared about you very much."

How could she explain to the loyal Mrs. Duncan when she did not herself understand her feelings, her sense of betrayal?

"He's going over the books." She smiled at the woman's cry of indignation.

"Whatever are ya letting 'im do that for?" Mrs. Duncan set her hands firmly on her ample hips.

Giving the protective woman a hug, Winter just shook her head. "I had no choice, Mrs. Duncan, but thank you for your confidence.

* * *

Winter was unaware of her beloved servants' concern for her, feeling only the pain in her own heart as the groom lifted her onto the sidesaddle.

Combing her fingers through the horse's soft mane, Winter glanced down at Mutton-head, who leaped up and down in excitement.

Gathering the reins, she urged the prime animal into an easy canter. Beside them, Mutton-head barked and zipped forward on four stubby legs.

The breeze whipped Winter's pale face. Her spirits needed purging and only a gallop would do. As though of his own volition, Jupiter turned up the forest path to the top of Renton Hill. Winter brought the gelding to a halt at the crest of the hill. From this vantage point she surveyed the whole of her domain. The farms and fields stretched out below her.

She had been so proud of her ability to manage the estate. Her father often complimented her. True, the work exhausted her meager strength, but it was hers. Her father loved her, she knew that. Then why, why? Why had he taken it all away from her by placing her in the care of a guardian?

She considered Lord Derik's proposal then dismissed it. Something about his proposal did not feel right. Besides, she could not imagine walking through life with a man for whom she held less than warm feelings. Then there was Lord Alistair. Lord Alistair was not the monster she first pictured, but what did he care about her wishes?

"Why, God?" she cried, flinging her head upward.

Staring straight ahead, Winter let the tears gather in her eyes and spill unheeded down her cheeks.

Closing the last ledger with a snap, Lord Alistair opened the drawer and dropped the heavy stack inside. Stretching, he got to his feet and swung about with an apologetic smile.

"Winter?" Frowning he growled. "Where did she go off to now?"

He tugged the bell cord with an impatient hand to summon the butler. "My lord. What can I do for you?"

"I wish to speak with Lady Renton."

"She's not here, my lord. She left sometime past."

Lord Alistair's frown deepened. "Left. Where did she go?"

"Lady Winter rode off on that horse of hers," the retainer answered. "The way she was ridin' only one place she be headin'—Renton Hill."

Annoyed, Lord Alistair curtly asked for directions. A few minutes later, he swung onto his Arabian-blooded roan stallion and cantered after his ward.

The girl would need to bow to his guardianship whether or not she desired his interference in her affairs. If only he could make her understand her father wished only for her protection.

Before he knew it, he emerged from the tree line on the crest of the hill. Winter's still figure stood silhouetted against the late afternoon sky. Pulling up, Lord Alistair studied the unmoving figure.

In her black riding habit, on her gray horse and with her silvery hair flowing softly around her, Winter made a lovely picture. Quietly, Lord Alistair urged the roan to her side.

Though Winter seemed completely unaware of him, a small mutt yipped at him sharply. Piqued at Winter's lack of acknowledgment, he leaned over and peered into her small oval face.

Only then did he witness her tears. They moved him as no other woman's tears ever had. Mayhap, he decided, it was because they were not accompanied by loud sobs, manipulative gestures or words. Winter's tears seemed torn from the depths of her being.

"Your books are in good order," he said. "Obviously you know what you're about." He paused.

Slowly Winter moved her head and stared over at him, her

lashes still wet with tears. The lost sadness in her eyes made Lord Alistair want to reach over and comfort her. Yet he kept his hands on the reins of his restless animal. Winter might take his gesture of assurance amiss and he did not want that, not after his less-then-gentlemanly insinuation when they first met.

"You really think I am a good manager?" She tangled her fingers in her horse's mane.

"I see no reason to change how you are handling things here."

"No manager?"

"No, no manager, at least for now."

"No nurse?"

Lord Alistair chuckled. "Certainly no nurse. I see no reason to throw money away."

"I thought you'd take it all away." Her quiet tone made her words all that more telling.

"It still belongs to you, Winter. My purpose is not to take your rights away, but to protect those rights." He cleared his throat. Winter's gaze did something strange to his insides.

As though a burden fell off her shoulders, Winter straightened. Taking a cambric square from her pocket, she wiped her eyes.

Lord Alistair cautioned, "I will, however, check in with you from time to time. After all, you are my responsibility until you marry."

He watched fear flash in her eyes. "You won't force me to marry?"

He hastened to reassure her. He paused as he patted the shoulder of his horse. "No. I only wish other women held such noble ideals." He thought of Amelia, the woman who'd taken his heart, caused a scandal and then married a peer with deeper pockets, leaving him cynical and bitter. "Keep those ideals, Winter."

She shot him a grin that all but stopped his heart. "Then you may be responsible for me for a very long time."

Lord Alistair grinned back. "I'll take my chances."

Suddenly Winter laughed, not the artificial laughter Lord Alistair so often heard in the genteel parlours of London, but the laugh of pure, unadulterated joy.

"Lord," he heard her soft whisper, "he's not going take everything from me. Thank You." Gratitude sparkled in her eyes. "Thank you, Lord Alistair...Justin."

Before he could respond, she wheeled the gelding and yelled, "Race you back to the stables."

For a moment, Justin watched the petite figure hunched forward over her horse's withers, her hair streaming out behind her.

Kicking his stallion into action, Lord Alistair raced after his ward, feeling younger than he had in a long time.

Chapter 3

The two horses rocketed into the stable yard in a dead heat. Laughing, Winter pulled up her mount and proceeded to walk him slowly until Jupiter's breathing eased. Beside her, Justin, too, cooled off his mount. As they pulled up, grooms ran out to hold the horses.

Swinging from the roan, Justin reached for Winter. Spanning her tiny waist with his large hands, he gently lifted her from the saddle and set her on her feet.

He smiled down at her with a boyish grin that caught her breath.

Blushing, she stepped away from the hands still holding her waist. "Jupiter is small, but he was born and bred as a racehorse."

"I'll remember that." Lord Alistair assisted her up the path to the wide steps of the colonnaded front of the manor. Duncan opened the door.

"Dinner usual time, m'lady?" He hesitated, then asked, "For two?"

Glancing up at her escort, Winter nodded. "I should have asked. Will you stay? I am sure that ride must have given you an appetite." Winter caught the approval in the old retainer's face and knew Duncan had accepted Lord Alistair as her rightful guardian.

At Justin's knowing grin in her direction, he knew it, too, and that irritated her. "Of course, it is getting late. If you must be on your way, I understand."

She knew her emotions chased themselves across her face for Lord Alistair to see. His grin flashed from Duncan to Winter. "Yes, I would be honored to stay. Thank you."

Despite her annoyance, Winter could not still the pleasure she felt at his acceptance. As Jenny from the village showed Lord Alistair up to a room in which to wash up, she hurried to her bedchamber.

Winter slid out of her dusty clothes and washed up. Mrs. Duncan held up her royal blue silk gown. "Here's a chance to wear that new gown we finished."

Winter added a white sash and white kid slippers. After Mrs. Duncan clasped a strand of pearls around Winter's neck, the older woman picked up a silver-backed brush and tackled Winter's tangled locks.

Pulling a blue ribbon from the drawer, the older woman tied it around Winter's hair. Winter smiled when the woman stood back with a contented sigh.

As Winter entered the parlour, she found Lord Alistair already there looking quite presentable after washing up and straightening his wilted cravat. His eyes widened with appreciation when he saw her. Only a slight hesitation in her gait gave evidence of her limp, and she hoped he wouldn't notice.

He bowed over her trembling hand. "You look lovely this evening, Lady Renton."

Winter pulled her hand from his grasp. She was relieved when the butler announced dinner.

"May I?" Taking her arm in his, Lord Alistair escorted her to the table for all the world, Winter thought, as though she were a lady of consequence.

His deference toward her throughout the many courses should have pleased her. Instead, she wondered how often he played the role, if indeed it was a role, of a practiced London dandy.

While they consumed the tender duck in a delicate mushroom sauce, he told her about his estate.

"Do you really like it?" she asked. "The food, I mean, not your estate."

"Best country food I've tasted in an age." He added, "Be thankful you have such a splendid cook. Not all that usual in the country. However, please don't tell that to my chef in London or he'll go off in a pique."

"We are blessed in that regard." Winter smiled.

"Mayhap you're right, Winter." His gaze rested on her with obvious appreciation. "I am blessed to partake with such a gracious, lovely companion."

Discomposed, she lowered her long lashes, shuttering her eyes from view. "I am sure you are fluent in your flattery, but it is unnecessary in my case."

Pausing, Lord Alistair's lips twisted cynically. "I don't waste my compliments or make them undeserved, I assure you."

Lord Alistair's return to his earlier sarcasm drained the joy Winter felt in his presence. Later, as his lordship sipped his wine, she felt his contemplative gaze on her. "You've gotten very quiet."

Winter glanced up. "I thought you might be angry with me."

Lord Alistair's eyebrow raised in surprise. "No, I am, in fact, quite glad to be here, enjoying this dinner with you. It certainly isn't what I contemplated when I came to see about my ward."

She tensed, her hand gripping her utensil. "What did you expect—a dim-witted child too disabled to know her own mind?"

Lord Alistair frowned. Putting down his wineglass with deliberation, he said, "How was I to know I would find, instead, a very lovely, self-assured young woman?"

Winter's lashes flickered momentarily over her eyes to hide the confusion in her heart at the compliment. "I see," Lord Alistair said as though he knew how she felt. His next words revealed how much he did know. "So you are unused to compliments. What a shame for such a lovely young woman to be hidden away in the country."

To distract her guardian from further flattery, Winter asked, "Tell me about yourself, Lord…ah, Justin."

Lord Alistair's long fingers on the stem of the goblet swished the last drops of wine in the glass as though debating what to say. "I have one brother, he's…" Again the hesitation. "He spent time in India." He stared at the Waterford crystal glass in his hand.

"After Mother died, Father decided to sail to India. He said he needed to get away from all the memories for a while. As you probably already know, his ship sank. No survivors."

"I know. I'm sorry." She reached out and touched Justin's arm.

Swallowing, he forced a smile as he covered her hand with his own. "So, I have the country seat, Stuart Park, the London town house, a hunting lodge in Scotland and other properties."

Feeling decidedly awkward, Winter extricated her hand. She felt they somehow spoke on two different levels, and she did not quite understand what was happening. "Are you expanding your farms to help in the war effort?" Her question diffused the situation. She sighed with relief. If he noticed, Lord Alistair let it go.

"Yes, and I noticed your new method of crop rotation. Has it increased the production of your farms?"

Winter grimaced. "Yes, once I convinced the farmers of the

wisdom of the plan. Of course, it's all new for us, and it is too early to see if the new system will benefit in the long-term."

"I don't think I've ever known farm matters to interest anyone of the female persuasion, with the exception of my mother." His gaze softened and Winter knew his mother came to mind.

"Well, I am certainly interested in preserving my nation. Should we have a full-scale war with Boney, we'll need all our resources."

"You don't think the truce will hold?" Lord Alistair leaned forward to hear her response.

"Do you? If war comes, what about all those foolish Englishmen who have gone to France thinking Napoleon has given up his plan to rule the world?"

A look Winter couldn't interpret crossed Lord Alistair's face as he spoke slowly. "I would like to think Boney will keep his word, but can't quite convince myself he will do so."

Deftly, and so quickly Winter glanced at him warily, he changed the subject. "Truthfully, I have been studying how to expand my own farming operation."

When Winter registered surprise, he said with chagrin in his tone, "Did you not consider that I might take my responsibilities to my estates seriously?"

Winter blushed. "I…ah…"

"I presume—" she heard the sarcasm in his tone as he continued and something more—pain "—you've only heard rumors. Seems you made as many judgments about me as I did about you."

"Mayhap." She cast about for a way to pick up the thread of their earlier topic. "About crop rotation…"

As though recognizing the wisdom in backing away, Lord Alistair said, "I've been reading up on it and what I discovered…"

As they spoke together, Lord Alistair shook his head. "I don't think I've ever known any woman as intelligent or as interested in farming as you," he told her. "I'm beginning to doubt, not for the first time, mind you, the prevailing wisdom spouting the 'fact' that females do not have the same capacity for reasoning as men. Obviously, those experts never met you."

He thought of Amelia, seeing her artificially red lips pout at him whenever he broached any subject other than herself, her arms reaching for him cloyingly. His expression hardened with the pain of his thoughts and Winter faltered midsentence.

"Justin?" she questioned.

With a start, Lord Alistair remembered Winter. "Excuse me. What did you say?"

Winter shook her head. "It wasn't important."

Her guardian caught her look of disappointment. Leaning forward, he took her hand in his. "I do tender my apologies. It was uncivil of me to let my mind wander. An old problem came to mind, and…"

Winter's hand trembled in his. "I know you're probably bored spending the evening talking about farming with a country girl, rather than cutting a dash in some London drawing room."

"Bored, no." He knew nothing but the truth would serve. "If you must know, I was thinking I have never really seriously conversed with a woman before, not like I've been discussing with you. I find it intriguing, not boring." He squeezed her hand and released it. "I'm talking to you like I would to a man…or a friend."

He let Winter search his face for the truth of the matter. "Friend. You mean that? I haven't had many friends."

"Then I trust you will count me as one."

"I'd like that, Justin." Winter's smile warmed Lord Alistair's heart.

As dinner drew to a close, Winter stood. "This is the time I should leave you to your port."

"Please. I have no desire for my own company tonight, and

less desire for port." Getting to his feet, he took her arm. "To the parlour, m'lady."

Later when Winter surreptitiously yawned behind her hand, Lord Alistair reluctantly stood. Taking her hand, he bowed. "Thank you for a most enjoyable evening, Winter."

She looked at him as though she suspected he jested. "Justin?"

"Whatever else you believe of me, Winter," he said, "I am truthful."

He was already taking his leave when the butler announced in disapproving tones, "Viscount Derik insists on seeing you, m'lady. He waits in the west parlour."

Sighing, she got up. Lord Alistair did not miss the annoyance that crossed her face. Discreetly, he followed her into the parlour.

Lord Alistair admired the way she straightened and focused on the haughty face of her would-be suitor. The viscount bowed smoothly, but Lord Alistair noticed he made no attempt to take her hand. "Winter, quite the thing tonight. I fully approve. Once we get you decked out in the latest Paris fashions..."

His flattery grated with insincerity. "Thank you, Anthony, but flattery is unnecessary and will not make me bend to your will one wit. Now why did you see the need to come here at this time of night?"

"If we could but sit down and talk things over." Lord Alistair tensed when the viscount touched her cheek.

"I think not, Viscount Derik." Winter's shoulders straightened. "It is far too late to deal with your interests tonight. What do you want?"

He smiled, but his smile did not reach his eyes. Still, Lord Alistair wondered if he was projecting his own concerns onto the man. "It is lonely here at Renton Hall, isn't it, Winter? Very isolated. Are you sure you are safe here? I am concerned." Lord Alistair saw Winter shiver. "Let me take care of you, Winter."

As Winter tensed, the viscount hurried on. "Think of it.

We'd deal well together, you and I. With our merging, as I said before, we would hold one of the largest estates this side of London. It is a chance to pass all this on to children, your children."

"I know you are overinterested in enlarging your estate, but…" Winter bit her lip. Lord Alistair bristled at the man's manipulation of the vulnerable young woman. The image of her being at his mercy in the most intimate of moments sent a chill down his spine.

Glancing up, Winter held the viscount's gaze. "I am sorry, Anthony, but believe I have already given you a clear response. I refuse to be a part of a marriage farce such as you propose. One without love. Why not choose some comely young woman who is being popped off this season?"

"I am more interested in someone who prefers the country." The viscount's lips thinned. "Besides, how can an unfledged chit like you hope to run this estate alone? Do you want me to make you love me?" His gaze narrowed. "I can do the pretty for you, if that is what you need…"

He would have said more, but Lord Alistair stepped out of the shadows. Putting his large hands on Winter's shoulders, he was surprised at her delicate bone structure.

The viscount took a step back at the earl's sudden appearance. "M'lord?"

"Viscount Derik."

"Lord Alistair, isn't it?" Lord Derik acknowledged grudgingly. His glance slid to Winter. "What is he doing here? I am certain he hasn't proposed marriage. He's not the marrying kind."

"Oh, be quiet, Anthony," she told him in the voice of one used to the antics of an old, if not always welcomed, childhood acquaintance. "Lord Alistair was just leaving. He is my guardian and trustee of the estate." The viscount's astonishment was almost worth the burden of the guardianship.

Lord Derik spluttered, "Your guardian?" He caught himself. "Your father must have been ready for Bedlam to do a thing like that!"

"Father was quite up to snuff, as you well know," Winter exhorted.

Lord Alistair surveyed the other gentleman. "In truth, Lady Renton can make no major decisions without my approval. That is the way things are, Lord Derik, and pressuring her will not make me favor your suit in my eyes or hers."

"Then persuade Winter of the truth of what I say. You know she can't stay here alone indefinitely."

"You think you're the only choice around?"

"In truth, yes."

Lord Alistair squeezed her shoulder lightly in reassurance. "My ward needs time right now. She is in mourning, but in time—" the words slipped out without thought "—a London season might be in order." Even as the words formed, he realized his responsibilities extended much further than he had considered. But this time, they didn't seem so burdensome.

"Viscount Derik, until that time, I suggest you leave off pressuring Lady Renton."

Lord Derik scowled. "I doubt you have shared your plans with her. She hasn't even been out to church since her father died. Do you not think her…her…problems will escape notice of the London tabbies? A London season is not for her."

Winter's head snapped up. "That is between Lord Alistair and myself, Anthony. Please. It is time for you to leave."

Without waiting for his reply, Winter turned and limped from the room.

At Lord Alistair's penetrating gaze, the viscount quickly took his leave. After making sure the man was indeed leaving, Lord Alistair followed Winter back to the salon in which they'd spent such a pleasant evening. He found Winter standing stiffly in front of the hearth, staring blindly into the flames.

Silently he peered into her tense face. Startled, her large

blue eyes beseeched his. "He is gone?" At his nod, she expelled a long slow breath. "Anthony can be overbearing at times."

For a long moment she remained silent, then asked, "Is he right about London? I do not desire a season." She sucked in a deep breath. "Must I really consult you before every decision?"

At this, Lord Alistair smiled. "Only major decisions. As for the other, we'll see. I want you to think of me as a friend to whom you'll go for help or advice."

His smile faded. "I do have a responsibility to keep in touch with you and to make certain you are taken care of and to make sure you not being harassed by the likes of Lord Derik."

Winter sucked in a deep breath. "Then you won't force me to marry him."

"Never! Too pompous by half."

"Quite." She grinned with relief.

"Satisfied, dear Winter?" Reaching for her hand he found it cold. "Trust me." After rubbing some warmth into her hand, he gently brought it to his lips. "Now, I really must take my leave. If ever you need anything, anything at all—send for me. Promise?"

"Promise." Winter tried to pass off the excitement she felt as his lips brushed her fingers. From his controlled actions, she could almost pretend her hands were not repulsive.

With a disquieting sadness, she watched him stride away. Even so, a strange joy welled up inside. He had not taken anything away. Though, if she were honest, she would have also admitted her joy came from the sure knowledge that she would see him again.

"Thank You, Lord, for Justin," she whispered, then softly smiled.

Chapter 4

Come live with me and be my love,
And we will all the pleasures prove.

Sitting back on the tapestried armchair by his desk, Lord Alistair glanced away from the sampler embroidered so many years ago by his great aunt when she was but a child. The poem reminded him of the previous night at Covent Gardens, where an actor quoted it.

His companion had been the green-eyed redhead, Lady Bridget. Throughout the performance she flirted with her mysterious eyes, with the warmth of her body next to his, and with the possessiveness of her hands.

Lord Alistair returned home alone, irritated and frustrated. He thought to break the tedium of his life since returning to London by escorting Lady Bridget around town. However, her lack of decorum grated on him in a way it might not have done before his evening in the company of Winter. Did Lady Bridget simply wish to sit in his pocket or to have something more permanent? He certainly did not see Bridget remaining faithful to him throughout the years, nor he to her. That gave him pause.

Winter was different from any woman he had met in London. His mother would have liked her. So, too, his aunt. Despite her problems, she exuded an inner strength, an inner joy that sparkled from her large blue eyes.

Since their encounter, his own life seemed like so much drudgery. Yet he knew, from his own experience, the mindless revelry of the young bucks with too much money and not enough sense also led to boredom and emptiness. Not that he completely cut himself off from the frivolities of the social world. Though his responsibilities lay heavy upon him, they did not keep him from occasionally putting his duties behind him. On the upper corner of his desk sat his latest invitation.

Lord Alistair bent his head over his work and forced himself to attend to his manager's latest requests. Two hours later he leaned back. Putting his morbid thoughts behind him, Lord Alistair strode up the wide staircase to his bedchamber. "I've decided to attend the prince at Carlton House tonight," he announced to his valet.

Instead of riding in state in his fine red-and-black carriage with a coachman, Lord Alistair drove his own phaeton with his tiger hanging on the back. He counted on a lighthearted evening with friends to divert his depressing reflections. The dinner at Carlton House, Prinny's residence and hub of his rakish social circle, would invariably contain courses too numerous and too rich to set comfortably.

"I'll just have to eat and drink sparingly," Lord Alistair told himself. Unlike many of his circle, he despised those who imbibed to the point of idiocy.

Then again, since debutantes were invited for the evening that would end in a ball, mayhap Prinny's more bawdy cronies—especially those most likely to tempt a husband-hunting mama—would absent themselves. He smiled to himself. If he stayed, he would take care not to fall into their clutches.

The majordomo announced Lord Alistair into the opulent hall, already crowded with ladies in costly gowns with scandalous décolleté and dripping in jewels, side by side with young women in modest virginal white and gentlemen in their own finest formal wear and jewels. As he sauntered into the room, the crowd parted to let him make his way unhindered to Beau Brummell, who stood by his friend and sponsor, the Prince of Wales, the next King of England. Both men effusively greeted Lord Alistair.

After properly greeting the Prince, Lord Alistair nodded toward London's fashion leader. "George."

Brummell scanned him bottom to top. "Nicely done. Not too much. Just enough." Grudgingly, he gave his approval to Lord Alistair's elegant but simple well-tailored turnout.

As expected, the dinner was a long drawn-out affair. The lady to his left simpered through each course. When she spoke disparagingly of the farmers, he coldly turned to the gentleman on his right only to, once again, find the gentleman totally engrossed in tipping his wineglass.

As the meal dragged on, Lord Alistair wondered why he ever thought to find diversion here. All around him he heard the latest on-dits, latest speculations, latest shallow comments that grated on his nerves. His lips twisted with cynicism as he thought of their response if they knew of his own involvement with the government affairs they spoke of so disparagingly and with such ignorance.

After dinner, when he would have excused himself, he found himself carried along to the ballroom. Sighing, Lord Alistair joined a group of well-dressed gentlemen, conversing quietly among themselves as they critically surveyed the couples on the floor.

"Alistair, good to see you again. Heard you were rusticating in the country." A beefy hand shook his.

"Lord Heywood."

Lord Heywood grimaced as he glanced toward the dance floor. "Look out there, Alistair. What do you see?"

Alistair viewed the young women dancing politely with their rather bored partners. "I see nothing unusual. A bevy of debutantes, desperately seeking wealthy, titled husbands, and the more dashing beaus flirting with the more available and less confining widows."

Lord Heywood chuckled. "Exactly so, Alistair. Look at those chits. Not an original among them."

Lord Sear, a thin gentleman who nervously tugged at his lapel, spoke up. "Still, they are lovely decked out in their finery."

"Ah, but all of the same mold," said Heywood. "I'll wager there isn't a chit among them who is educated in more than manipulating her way to the altar. What do they care the treaty is disintegrating, and soon Boney will be at our throats once more?"

Alistair glanced around the room. "Since the Treaty of Amiens last year, most of our countrymen assume Napoleon has become respectable."

Lord Heywood snorted. "Once a conqueror, always a conqueror. He won't be satisfied for long."

Sear nervously fingered the glass in his hand. "Serious about a unique entry into this season's marriage mart, Heywood? A serious wager?"

"Right and tight." Lord Heywood grinned. "I'll put up a thousand pounds just to see a unique, intelligent woman popped off."

"Intelligent?" Alistair's thoughts turned to Winter. "Just what are you looking for?"

"Well, let's see. Someone who doesn't ape this crowd. Someone not out just for a warm body with deep pockets and a title."

Sear frowned. "Heywood, that's the whole reason those

chits are in London. Their parents don't lay out hundreds and hundreds of pounds just for them to have a good time."

"You want a bluestocking?" This from Alistair.

"Spare me, Alistair. I said intelligent, not badly turned out. No, I am looking for someone who wants more. Someone who looks beyond herself. And," he added, "the chit absolutely must not simper or giggle at every word spoken to her."

"My, my." Lord Sear shook his head. "Don't ask much, do you? Just who is to be the judge of this paragon?"

Heywood puffed out his barrel chest. "Myself, of course. After all, it is my pockets to let if someone produces this original."

"The season has already started. How long do we have?"

"A week or so, mayhap."

"There you are, Justin." Lady Bridget, having just arrived, possessively looped her arm through his. "Come. Time to leave your stuffy conversation."

Reluctantly, he allowed her to drag him away from his friends, his mind already busy with a very interesting idea.

She tried to focus his wondering attention on herself. "How long have you been back in London? I haven't seen you about."

"I've been busy," he grunted in response.

"Was your trip excessively dreary? Poor man, having the burden of some dimwit on your hands."

Laconically, Alistair smiled into her jealous green eyes that suddenly reminded him of cat's eyes. "Not so dreary after all, Bridget."

A light shown in his eyes as he thought of his innocent ward. He only later realized his companion thought the warmth of his eyes was for her.

Unique, thought Alistair. *Heywood demands unique.* He envisioned the unpretentious Winter done up in the new simple-but-fashionable style, her gorgeous hair rippling down her back.

Of course, why not bring Winter to London? How many

even knew how long ago Lord Renton died? To own the truth, she needed to get out of the country and meet someone more suitable than Lord Derik.

Though he had not attempted to contact her since leaving her and returning to London a couple of weeks earlier, he had not been able to get her from his mind. High time he made a visit. High time he brought her to London.

Meeting and parting with Bridget in the minuet, Alistair's thoughts remained on his ward. He noted Lady Bridget's attempts to get his attention and pulled back when she pressed her sensuous body against his. He wondered, not for the first or tenth time, about her motivation for seeking him out. From the on-dits at his club, she seemed less than ready to settle down, and yet her hints were too specific not to make him think elsewise. He needed to take care or he'd find himself leg-shackled. He eased away from her clinging arms.

The next morning Alistair climbed into his carriage, an elegant, well-sprung red-and-black vehicle with the family coat of arms emblazoned on the doors, and let the coach carry him to Renton Hall.

Not until he stopped for the night at a posting-house did Lord Alistair realize he had not considered bringing along a lady's maid or a chaperone for Winter.

"Surely she can find someone to travel with her," he told himself, then frowned. Not having a chaperone on the journey could easily cause a scandal and ruin Winter's chances in London.

The next morning, rested and eager to be on his way, Alistair climbed into the carriage. After the footman closed the door, Alistair laid his head back, his expression softening at the thought of Winter's large blue eyes and silvery hair.

The past couple of weeks had gone swiftly for Winter, who stayed busy overseeing the tenantry, the farms and cottages, the household, gardens, parkland, paddocks and stables. For the first time, she began to admit the load was indeed a heavy one to bear. Even when her father was ill, he had been there to advise.

Warmer weather brought forth the old rivalry between the farmers Jones and Andrews, and she rode out to find them yelling at each other.

Jones growled, "'Tis mine to farm this year."

Andrews countered, "You had this strip of ground last year."

"Turn and turn about. That's what the old lord told us, and it's my year."

Seeing her, they nodded stiffly and tersely claimed the right to farm the small strip of land between their farms that had been a point of contention for years.

"Did not my father say each of you could use the land on alternating years?" Jupiter shifted restlessly under her tight rein. "So what is the problem?"

"Jones here was sick last year, and I farmed the land," Andrews told her. "Now he claims the right to it this year."

Winter asked, "That's a problem?"

"Not for me." Jones shrugged. "What difference, one year to the next?"

Andrew leaned on his hoe. "Ah, but my lady, I was trying that rotation system of yours. I need this year to balance out last."

"Very good, Andrews."

Jones protested. "I need the land, as well, m'lady. Martha is increasing again and we need the income."

Glancing toward the neat cottages, Winter spied the wives of the men standing close together, their hands clasped. She sighed, frustrated at the continued fighting between the men over such an insignificant parcel of land.

Wheeling Jupiter, she rode up to the women. "Martha, congratulations. Jane."

A smile of pleasure crossed the faces of the women, who curtsied awkwardly. "M'lady."

Jane stepped forward. "I am sorry they are at it again. We tried to stop them."

"As though," Martha grumbled softly, "they are the only ones without enough land."

Winter straightened. "What do you mean?"

"Why, m'lady," Jane said. "Between us we have barely a spot of garden large enough to feed our—" she grinned slyly at her friend before continuing "—growing families."

"I see." Winter knew the women were not only long-time friends, but cousins, as well. An idea formed all of a piece. "There is no need to brangle about this. I know what to do!"

Motioning the men to her side, she declared, "From now on this contested land will be shared equally."

The two men glared at one another. The women sighed.

"You don't understand." Winter smiled toward the wives. "From now on Martha and Jane, this is yours to garden together."

She was rewarded with the smile and fumbled gratitude from the two women while the men took it in more slowly. The excitement of their wives decided them.

Jones scratched his head. "Well I'll be."

Andrews agreed. "Done right well, m'lady. His lordship be proud, he would."

Winter blinked back tears as she accepted their thanks. Not until she was out of sight, did she let her shoulders droop in exhaustion. She had thought to handle everything herself, but it was getting to be too much. Mayhap it was time to find an estate manager, but… Her pride alone kept her working without the interference of a manager.

Her thoughts turned, as they often did, to her tall, commanding guardian. Mayhap he could find her a manager. "No," she said aloud, "I will not give him cause to doubt my abilities. Besides, he has probably all but forgotten me."

That thought did not cheer her as she had intended.

Truth to tell, her loneliness grew with each passing day.

As she passed through the wood, she heard the twittering of the birds as they set up their nests, watched one rabbit follow another across the path.

She thought of Duncan and his wife, but, however dedicated they were to her, they had each other and their family.

She had only one friend and to him she had insisted she needed no one but herself. After only two weeks, she was finding self-sufficiency decidedly uncomfortable, especially where Viscount Derik was concerned.

Several times he had dropped by on one pretext or another. Once he was looking for a horse, another time he complained of a downed fence. Always he was arrogant, and always assumed that sooner or later Winter would be forced to accept him.

She found him waiting for her when she returned home. At his condescending smile, she rubbed her forehead, feeling the headache start as it had been wont to do of late whenever she dealt with the viscount.

"Not today, Anthony. I don't wish to argue with you today."

"Fine. Don't argue." Impatiently, he tapped his riding boots with his riding crop. "Just agree you'll have me. If you agree, I am certain that your guardian, who seems less than interested in your welfare, will be glad to get out from under his obligation."

His statement so closely mirrored Winter's own assessment, she winced. Her head pounded and her eyes blurred with exhaustion—or was it tears? "No. And again, no! I do not love you. I do not even like you, and I certainly will not marry you. Not now, not ever."

When he reached for her, she stepped back and rang for Duncan. "You have overstepped all bounds of propriety with your continual visits."

He smiled sardonically. "Who's going to stop me?"

Winter shivered under his threat. "Oh, Anthony. Go, please."

The butler, standing in the open doorway, cleared his throat. Frowning, Anthony took the hint.

"I won't wait forever, Winter. I have plans for you…for us. You *will* marry me." With that the viscount pivoted smartly and strode confidently from the room.

Winter felt the bars of his cage closing over her. Brushing aside the feeling, she left the room for the study, where, one by one, she hauled out the different ledgers.

Opening one at random, she buried herself in book-work in order to bury also the viscount's threat. After an hour or so, she closed the book with a snap. She ached from head to toe.

Though the sun had not yet hit its zenith, Winter felt she'd already worked a full day, and she wasn't far wrong. Fingering her dusty Bishop's blue habit, she decided that a warm bath and a change of clothing before luncheon would not be amiss.

Purposefully, she set the ledgers back into the drawer and closed it, before leaving the room. She met Duncan in the hallway.

"Duncan, would you have someone draw me a bath."

"Very good, m'lady, but you have a visitor. I put 'im in the east parlour."

Winter's heart sank. "A visitor. Not Lord Derik again."

"No, m'lady. Saw 'im out myself." She didn't miss the satisfaction in his eyes.

"Then it must be Lord Nelson. Probably his usual once a week pilgrimage."

"No, m'lady."

Her face brightened. "The reverend? Haven't seen him since father died."

"No, m'lady. In the parlour."

Irritated at his unusual reticence, Winter struggled with hostility, born of the depletion of her strength, pricking at her. All she needed was one more dubious and insulting proposal.

With effort, Winter straightened and attempted to walk slowly and gracefully, but gave up. She was just too exhausted to disguise her limp, for her leg was always weakest when she was tired. It did not bode well for her visitor.

Entering the open, heavily carved double doors, Winter stopped. "Lord Alistair?"

Hearing the lilt of welcome, he grinned, and she blushed. He made her acutely aware of her dusty skirt and mud-splashed riding boots.

Instinctively, she smoothed her skirt and limped toward him, her fury rising under his steady gaze. "You don't have to look at me like that," she complained, then bit her lip.

"Like what?" he asked. "As if you were a nymph rising from the sea, her moonlit hair streaming behind her, cheeks kissed by the breeze?"

Winter stared. "What! I thought... Oh, never mind."

Alistair raised her hand to his lips as he looked down into her face. Gently, he traced the tired lines etched under her eyes. "I was not mocking you, my dear Winter."

His gentleness brought tears to her eyes, and she sniffed to keep from crying. Her anger faded. Why did he have to show up when she looked so dreadful?

She allowed him to lead her to the settee, where he sat down next to her. "Is everything all right? You look tired."

"I am." Winter closed her eyes to hide the tears sparkling in them. Before she considered, Winter poured out her frustrations. Suddenly, she halted midsentence. Lord Alistair would think her a peagoose for prosing on.

Worse, her eyes widened, he'd think she was incompetent to handle her affairs. "Pardon. I'm tired, and not myself this morning. It's just one of those days." She tried to smile. "God is so good to me, and I shouldn't complain. M'lord, it's just..."

"What is this 'm'lord' balderdash? Didn't you agree to call me Justin?"

"I am sorry, Justin." She lowered long lashes over shimmering eyes. "I am glad you came."

"Hmm. Why is that?" He put a comforting arm around her shoulders.

"You're the only one who doesn't make demands of me," Winter told him.

Alistair cleared his throat. "Winter, I..."

She glanced up sharply. "What is it?" Her ire rose, along with her tone. "Planning on interfering with how I run my estate? Or is there some nurse in the offing?"

"Of course not!" He touched her cheek. "But you are over-tired. Obviously running the estate alone has taken its toll."

"I've thought of getting a steward, but where do I look?"

"Why didn't you contact me?"

Winter looked away. Putting his hand under her chin, he forced her to face him. "You are too stubborn for your own good, Winter. Now you are run-down. There is only one thing to do."

"What's that?" she whispered.

"Come back to London with me."

"Fustian! Have you bats in the cockloft? I'm still in mourning." She felt quarrelsome.

Alistair eyed her jutting chin. "Mayhap we could speak of this further after luncheon. You did say you wished to bathe and change."

"Did Duncan mention luncheon or did you invite yourself?"

At his silence, Winter momentarily closed her eyes. When she opened them, regret shimmered in their depths. "I'm sorry. Of course you must stay."

A smile played at the corners of his lips. "Since I am your guardian, Duncan assumed I would be asked to dine with you."

At his gentle reproof, Winter flushed. "He's right. You're right." Her shoulders slumped.

"Let's talk then, after luncheon."

Slowly Winter shook her head. "No, I'd rather discuss it now. Not that there is much to say. I may accept a manager, but I am not going to London."

"I plan on presenting you into London society." Alistair couldn't miss the obstinate light dawning in Winter's eyes.

"You what? I know you suggested this on your previous visit, but this is outside of… I'm no simpering society miss."

"Exactly so," Alistair agreed.

She spoke scathingly. "I am certainly not interested in being paraded in London's 'marriage mart.'"

Alistair's silence fueled her frustrated anger. "Look at me, Justin. Look at me. No London beau would be interested in me. I have no desire to be part of the wasteful extravagance of society, wear positively indecent gowns or have my hair done up in some impossible coiffure. Then there is the behavior of the gentlemen themselves." Recalling her guardian's own scandal, she lowered her eyes.

Alistair's voice was low with annoyance. "You are speaking of men like myself, mayhap?"

Color rushed to her cheeks, and Winter kept her lashes lowered. "Yes, I suppose. Like you. I've heard about your…"

"Affair." Alistair threw up his hands. "Who hasn't?" He told her cynically, "It was the favored tittle-tattle of London, of all England, I suppose. Oh, and how the rumors grew with the telling. I suppose you think me a dreadful rake?"

Winter nodded with reluctance. Silence stretched between them. When Winter finally looked at him, her misery seemed to ease the tension of his expression. "I am so sorry. I did not mean to hurt you or bring to mind what causes you such pain."

"It's all right, Winter."

"Father did not approve of the Carlton House set, and I don't think—aside from the fact I am still in mourning—he would approve of me going to London…." Again she saw her mistake too late.

"With me," he finished. "Look, Winter. I don't consider myself one of Prinny's dissolute cronies. Further, I do not consider myself a rake, despite the things you've heard to the contrary." He forced her to face him. "Are you afraid of me? Do you believe I would do anything to dishonor you?"

Winter shook her head. "No, I am not afraid of you, Justin."

"Since your father placed you in my care, do you believe he intended for you to obey me as you did him?"

Her grin was sheepish. "I wasn't always very good at that, either. At least until the accident. I suppose he would."

"Then I am asking you to come to London. As your guardian, I think it is time you stop rusticating and get the bronze of a town season. The season is already under way and I want you to be part of it."

"But I am in mourning."

"Who's to know whether your father died five months ago or a year ago, unless we tell them? Your father hadn't ventured out of the country for years. I imagine few even took notice of his death, and fewer yet the date."

"The estate?" She grasped at any reason to stay, safe and secure in the country.

"Now don't fly up in the bough, but I've already asked Jonas to check things out. He's a good, honest, hardworking man. Since before my father's death, he has been working with my own comptroller and has some understanding of the situation."

"I haven't proper clothes. As for transparent gowns, forget them." She tugged the hair streaming in a tangled mass over her shoulders. "I refuse to cut my hair. So, see, I can't do as you ask. I'd embarrass you dreadfully."

Alistair chuckled. "Don't you realize that the gown you wore that first time I saw you was not much different from the latest London rage? You can dress with style and elegance without being indecent, Winter."

"But…"

"As soon as we get to London, you'll be fitted with a suitable wardrobe." He surveyed her trim, maturing figure. "Any modiste from Bond Street would be delighted to have you as her customer."

Winter willed herself not to flush, but failed. Why was Alistair so able to bring the color to her cheeks?

"My traveling coach awaits us outside. I assure you, Winter, you will be most comfortable at Alistair House on Berkeley Square."

"Alone with you?"

Anger darkened his eyes. "Can you not credit me with at least a particle of sense? That would put the kiss of death on your presentation."

He continued, "Before I left London I sent word to my aunt, the Dowager Duchess Ramsdale, my father's sister. She should arrive even before we do. If I know her, she'll be delighted with the opportunity to present a lovely young woman to the ton. Trust me, if she accepts you, so will the haute ton."

Winter glanced from her trembling hands to her guardian's stern face. "There is no choice involved, is there?"

"No, there isn't. I have decided it is best for you, but I had hoped you would not fight me on this. Doesn't the thought of a season please you in the least?"

Winter rubbed her aching forehead. She felt tired, too tired to fight Alistair any longer.

"I am afraid." The truth tumbled from her tired lips before she could pull the words back.

The surprise mirrored on Alistair's expression showed how much her honesty caught him off guard. "Afraid, of me?"

"No, of, of…"

"Of ridicule," prompted Alistair, understanding dawning in his eyes.

She nodded. Alistair took her trembling hand in his. "I am a man of consequence, Winter. They will not say aught when I am with you, and I promise to be your escort for as long as you need me. And, of course, my aunt is beyond reproach."

Her hand felt secure in his. Her trembling eased. "If I must go, I will be most grateful for your protection, and hers."

He grinned. "Then it is settled. Have Mrs. Duncan pack only a few necessities. We can leave directly after we eat."

"Could I ride Jupiter one last time?"

"Mayhap, if there is time before luncheon, but aren't you tired?"

She smiled. "A relaxing ride is just the thing."

"Without my roan I can't ask a rematch, but I do claim the privilege of riding with you."

"I'd like that, but I must tell you Jupiter is the best horse in the stable." Her voice grew sad. "I'll miss Jupiter."

"Not too much, I think." Alistair grinned. "I plan on having him brought to London."

"You'd do that for me! Thank you." She smiled. "Mayhap it won't seem so bad with Jupiter with me."

"Now, as to our traveling arrangements. I have rooms booked at the Dove for tonight. You'll need a lady's maid along, of course, and a companion."

Winter frowned. "Mrs. Duncan can't leave. She's also the housekeeper now. The village girls, well, they're rather awkward around me." A glint of triumph flashed in her eyes. "I guess that means I'll have to stay put. Sorry."

"Minx." Alistair's expression hardened with determination. "If I have to play lady's maid myself, my dear Winter," he told her, "you will come with me to London."

She gave in with ill grace. "There is Polly, Mrs. Duncan's daughter. She's helped me before, but she can't stay permanently. She's married and has two little ones."

"Don't worry. I'll send her back as soon as you are safely at Alistair House."

Winter teased, "I trust you'll be a gentleman."

Alistair glanced at her, a slight frown on his face. "In your eyes I am, of course, a totally dissolute character, yet you trust me to be a gentleman with you. Why is that?"

Twisting under his scrutiny, she said, "I meant no disrespect, Justin. I just know you wouldn't think of me in those terms."

With deliberation he drew her close, causing her heart to pound and her palms to sweat. "Why is that?"

"Because I...am...like this." She held up her hands.

Releasing her, he softened his voice. "Fustian! I warn you, such assumptions could lead you into serious trouble. You are a very lovely young woman."

At his start, Winter knew he'd witnessed both surprise and fear in her wide-eyed gaze. "I am your guardian, Winter. I will not only be the perfect gentleman, but I will also make sure to protect you from any unwanted advances."

"Like Lord Derik? He hasn't given up."

"Then it is high time you leave him behind."

"I'll be glad to forget him." Inside she had a feeling the viscount would not give up so easily.

Chapter 5

Alistair, his hand on Winter's elbow, led her into the parlour where his aunt, the Dowager Duchess Ramsdale, awaited them.

Tired, Winter paused, her gaze sweeping the tall, stately woman who carried herself with a dignity Winter could only hope to obtain. Her insides quaked as Alistair halted her before the formidable woman.

Bowing, Alistair smiled and greeted the woman before directing her attention to Winter. "Aunt Helen, my ward Lady Winter Renton. Lady Renton, my aunt, the Duchess of Ramsdale."

"Your grace." Winter executed the best curtsy of which she was capable.

Winter's chin jutted out as the woman silently took her measure. "So this is Lady Renton."

When Winter met her perusal without flinching, a smile quirked the woman's generous lips. "La, I think she will do. She'll do nicely, Justin."

Alistair smiled his reassurance. "She likes you." He chuckled.

An angry flush tinged Winter's cheeks at the knowing look in the older woman's eyes. The odious man!

"It's all right, child. Of a certain I like you…as Justin knew I would." Her low musical laughter reassured Winter far more than Alistair's teasing.

"You may not become the reigning belle of the season, but…" Putting her hands on Winter's shoulders, she slowly turned her about. "Once we get you into some of Rose Bertin's creations…"

"Aunt Helen," Alistair interjected, "I don't believe Bertin is the right modiste for Winter's delicate beauty. I will not have her turned into a copy of every other chit on the market."

He ignored the flash in Winter's eyes at the veiled reference to the marriage mart. "She needs a softer image. No revealing décolletage and no silly coiffures."

He added, "We're not cutting her hair, Aunt Helen. No fussy curls."

The duchess took this in with a lifted eyebrow. "Hmm. I see. Mayhap, yes, I believe you are right. There is a new modiste who recently opened shop. Young, ambitious and French. Might be just the one to help us launch your ward."

"I don't want to be any trouble," Winter said.

The duchess raised her eyebrows. "Modest and all that. Very good. Well, you're no trouble. I'd like to try her myself. Won't hurt her business to be patronized by the Earl of Alistair."

Alistair grinned. "Or the Duchess Ramsdale."

The duchess had not finished. "Your gown, child. Who designed it? Hasn't the dash of a French creation, but it suits you well."

Winter flushed. "Thank you, your grace. I designed it and my housekeeper sewed it."

"A practical young woman. Quite the rarity, I assure you." There was a slight bite to the words, and Winter was not sure whether or not the duchess approved. "Enough of that. It has been a long journey."

At Alistair's direction Winter gratefully sat down in a gracefully curved Hepplewhite settee covered in grass-green silk. Glancing over the mantelpiece, Winter noted the van Dyke painting.

Following the direction of her gaze, Alistair said, "The Second Earl of Alistair."

"I see the resemblance." She looked from the painting to her guardian and back again. "I always liked the way van Dyke caught detail with such accuracy."

She did not miss the light of approval in the eyes of the duchess, or Alistair's chuckle. "I told you, Aunt Helen, almost a bluestocking."

Winter flushed, but her anger faded as the duchess's gaze met hers with understanding. "A bluestocking in the old definition surely, Justin."

Seeing the flush on Winter's cheek, Alistair back-stepped. "Of a certain. I meant simply that you have a mind and use it. I like that."

The butler entered with a tray that he deftly set before the duchess. Winter's cheeks again blossomed when her stomach reacted noisily to the repast set before them. She stuttered an apology, which Alistair halted by handing her a mug of chocolate.

"My fault for not taking the time to stop again. After the delay caused by that wheel, I thought we should push for London."

Leaning back, Winter gratefully sipped from her mug while Alistair and his aunt conversed. The duchess regaled him with the latest on-dits while Alistair asked sharply about the eminent collapse of the truce with France. Their words eddied around Winter, becoming increasingly indistinct and blurred.

"Winter! Winter, wake up." Her head snapped up at Alistair's piercing command.

"Ah, oh. I'm sorry." She blinked sleep from her eyes.

Alistair chuckled. "No, my apologies to you. I should have realized how tired you were after two days of travel."

With a mischievous twinkle in his eyes, he added, "No matter how comfortable a bed at a posting-inn, it is certainly not like sleeping at home."

"We'll take care of that," said the duchess. "I have her room made up."

Winter stifled a yawn. "I admit to being exhausted."

Standing up, Alistair drew her to her feet. "If—" he nodded toward his aunt as he spoke "—you will excuse us, Aunt Helen…" With that, he personally escorted Winter from the room.

Lord Alistair left Winter in the care of his housekeeper. The thin, efficient woman in a rustling black dress promptly showed Winter the rose-colored room and supervised the hanging of the few clothes Mrs. Duncan had packed for her.

A young maid helped Winter change from her serviceable brown traveling suit into her worn but comfortable blue robe. Smiling, Winter dismissed the young girl, who didn't appear to be much over fourteen.

Though fatigued, Winter was not yet ready to lie down. Instead, she meandered around the large room, relishing the feel of the soft Aubusson carpet under her bare feet.

Running her hands over the cool silky rose drapes, Winter gazed out the tall windows that overlooked a lush lawn, sloping away in the distance. Straining, she could make out the dark outlines of some buildings she assumed comprised the stables.

"I wonder long it will be before Jupiter arrives."

Turning from the window, she studied the paintings on the walls. As she moved from one to the other, she came to the unmistakable conclusion, "Why, they all appear to be Rembrandts. How odd they all hang in the same room." She tucked the question away to ask Justin later.

Yawning, she gathered up her bible, which had been laid out on the nightstand, sat down on the bed and opened it to

Psalms. She needed the comfort of the familiar passages with her tonight.

The last two verses from Psalm 4 stuck in her heart.

Thou hast put gladness in my heart,
More than in the time that their corn and their wine increased.
I will both lay me down in peace and sleep:
For thou, Lord, only makest me dwell in safety.

Winter slowly closed the bible, blew out the bedchamber candle and snuggled under the covers. "Yes, Lord, thank You for keeping us safe."

The large four-poster bed enfolded her in its welcoming depth. She snuggled even farther under the warm covers until they all but covered her face. Feeling like royalty, she idly wondered if indeed some prince or princess ever slept in this room. It was her last thought before she slept.

Winter awoke with a groan to find a young maid in her room lighting the candles. Of medium height, the dark-haired young woman moved with a grace Winter envied. "M'lady?"

Winter yawned and smiled sleepily as the maid bustled about readying a bath in front of the fireplace. "Why are you getting me up in the middle of the night?"

The maid stilled a grin. "M'lady, you have slept the day away."

"I what!" The maid's eyes held the truth. "Oh, my."

Groaning, Winter got up, rubbing her aching thigh and slowly working her stiff joints. The days of traveling had exhausted her more than she realized. Hobbling over to the tub, Winter sank contentedly into the warm, scented water and let herself relax.

"Did Polly get off all right?"

"The woman who came with you? Yes, she did. Would have

said goodbye, but she didn't wish to disturb you. I'll be your personal abigail from now on."

Winter watched the young woman's graceful movements and heard her cultured speech. Even an impoverished gentlewoman did not usually become a servant, not if she was able to become a governess or companion.

Her curiosity overcame her hesitance. "Why?"

Her new abigail did not pretend to misunderstand. "My parents had to flee from the persecution in France. They were thankful to escape with their lives."

"Were you born here in England?"

"Yes, soon after they arrived, in fact."

"That accounts for your lack of accent." Winter paused.

The abigail smiled. "I am thankful to have honest work. Many French women have taken to the stage or…worse." She bit her lip.

"What do I call you?"

"Mary will do fine."

"Mary? Not Maria?"

"Actually, yes, it is Maria, but we thought it best to seem as English as possible."

Winter assumed she referred to her parents. "Are your parents also employed by his lordship?"

"Oh, no, m'lady, but—" she dimpled as she continued "—he did hire my husband as a groom, as well." There was a look in her eyes that Winter was unable to interpret.

"How long have you been married?"

"Eight months, m'lady." The water growing cold, Winter permitted Mary to help her from the bath.

"Congratulations."

A soft light shone in Mary's eyes. "Thank you, m'lady."

Winter focused on drying herself. While she did not wish Mary any less happiness, it brought a pain to Winter's lonely heart.

With a soft sigh, Winter dropped the towel and let Mary assist her into a clean shift and petticoats. Winter relaxed while Mary brushed out her hair in long smooth strokes. Pulling up the sides, Mary braided them around Winter's head with a rose-colored ribbon, leaving the rest flowing down her back in soft rippling waves.

The abigail brought out a gown Winter had never seen before. "Where did that come from?"

"Her grace did some shopping on her own for you this afternoon."

"How kind of her!" exclaimed Winter, who had secretly been worried about embarrassing her guardian with her country clothes. "I'll be sure to thank her."

Mary carefully lowered the gown over her head and tied the white sash. Staring at Mary in the mirror, Winter shook her head in amazement. "This gown makes me look so, so…"

"Refined."

"That's the word. You're a wonder. Thank you."

"My pleasure, m'lady. Let me show you the way downstairs. I am certain his lordship is waiting."

James, the pompous butler, stiffly showed Winter to the parlour off the long dining hall. Done in shades of brown, the room showcased several fine Fragonards.

"Winter." She looked up to find Alistair standing beside her.

"I'm sorry, Justin. I didn't see you. You look magnificent." Her cheeks flushed, and she covered them. All she did was blush around her guardian, but he did look wonderfully handsome in formal blue jacket and white breeches.

"I didn't mean to sleep all day."

"You needed the rest. Besides, once Aunt Helen takes over, you will thank me you got some rest first. A season is seldom conducive to much sleep." He followed her gaze. "You appreciate my paintings?"

"I do. I can't get over how many different and valuable paintings you have. I love Renton Hall. After all, it is my home, but this…" She indicated the luxurious paintings and furnishings.

Lord Alistair chuckled. "My ancestors spent a great deal of effort acquiring works of art." He motioned toward the valuable compositions. "They entailed them so that even if an heir needs the money, he cannot sell the family treasures. They can only be passed on to his son and heir."

"How strange it would be to starve in the midst of this wealth because your ancestors wanted to preserve this beauty."

"Almost funny, isn't it? It has happened to more than one family when they lost their money, often at the baize tables." At the look on Winter's face, he reassured her. "Have no fear, dear Winter. I am quite deep in the pockets so you must not be concerned about this peer. Wonder what's keeping Aunt Helen?"

"Before she arrives, I have a question."

"At your service, m'lady."

"Upstairs in my room are several Rembrandts, here there is not one, but several Fragonards. Last night the room we were in held several van Dykes. Are all the rooms like this with the works of the individual painters grouped together? Why?"

"Grandfather started it. He liked to study the differing styles at his leisure and hated mixing them. So, instead of having the blue or red room, we have the van Dyke parlour, the Stubbs study, the Rembrandt bedchamber. He was the same about furniture, but we've gotten away from that somewhat."

Winter laughed. "I see. It is rather simple after all. Oh, and I wanted to thank you for Mary. She is delightful."

Alistair smiled and Winter got the distinct impression he was secretly amused by her remarks. "I thought you might like her. Not exactly a bluestocking," he teased, "but she is well-educated."

He turned as the duchess walked toward them. "There you are, Aunt Helen."

James chose that moment to announce dinner. Giving an

arm to each, Alistair escorted the two women into the dining parlour.

Winter's hair, sparkling silver in the light from the gold candelabrum on the table, caught Lord Alistair's eye. Watching him, his aunt commented, "Always did think a woman looked her best in candlelight. None of those garish oil lamps for me."

That launched the duchess and her nephew into a discussion, bordering on an argument, regarding the latest inventions coming into fashion. Winter, glad for their diversion, ate whatever was set before her.

At one point, finding Alistair's intense gaze focused on her, Winter became so discomfited she dropped her utensil, which clattered against her gold plate.

"Justin," the duchess addressed him sternly, "can't you see you are making the child nervous?"

A laconic smile spread across his face as he glanced from Winter to his aunt and back again. "My most humble of apologies, Winter. Don't let my quiet observation cast you into the dismals."

"Don't concern yourself," Winter managed to say with a false sweetness he could not help but detect. "I'd hardly let the sight of you trouble me so."

The duchess gulped, choked back a snicker. "That's one for your ward, Justin. She may not be as they say, 'up to snuff' yet, but she will be soon. I predict she'll be an original, and I plan to take my share of the credit."

Winter finally relaxed and listened to the two wrangle. In time, she even interjected a comment or two.

There was no doubt her guardian believed that any day they would hear that Napoleon no longer had a truce with England. He spoke with such authority, Winter asked, "Did you ever fight the French?"

"Not exactly." He exchanged a look with the duchess she could not interpret, and changed the subject.

Biting her lip, Winter glared down at her plate. Already in her short stay, she intercepted strange looks, silences, or, like this instance, times her guardian changed the subject. What could it mean?

She missed the start of the new topic on the merits of French émigrés returning to France to regain their inheritance from Napoleon.

"It's all a farce," the duchess claimed. "How can you trust that Corsican? Contrary to many of my contemporaries, I wonder what's he going to do next?"

"I'd rather have the émigrés return to their homeland than to remain here as Boney's spies." Alistair's voice took on a hard edge.

"Spies?" Winter paled. "Why would they spy for the French government? After all, England gave them sanctuary when their own people were trying to murder them."

Alistair sadly shook his head. "I fear that it has already happened and much more is suspected."

"Mary?"

Again that look passed between the duchess and her guardian. "No, not Mary." He explained, "She married an Englishman and has set solid roots down into our country. As far as she is concerned, she is English and has proved herself a loyal citizen."

Winter wondered how, but Alistair's expression forbade further inquiry.

"Time we leave you to your port, Justin." The duchess rose gracefully.

Winter leaned forward and tried to emulate the graceful movements of the duchess but failed. As usual, her leg stiffened from the long sit, and it took several steps before she walked normally.

Behind her, she heard the grate of the chair as her guardian also rose. "I never cared for sitting alone. I prefer the company of lovely ladies."

"I'll wager you do," the duchess said with a chuckle that disheartened Winter, though she did not know why.

"You two go along. It has been a long day for me." She smiled at Winter. "I've made a lot of plans for the next few days, and we'll be very busy getting you ready for your presentation. I think I'll retire for the night so I'll be ready first thing in the morning."

Alistair tucked Winter's hand in the crook of his arm and led her down the hall to the library. Immediately, the warmth and security of the room surrounded her; though, if she were honest, she would have admitted it also had to do with the broad-shouldered man at her side.

"I thought we'd spend the evening here. It is my favorite room in the whole place."

Winter loved the room on sight. The heavy mahogany desk, with its clean ornamented lines, caught her gaze as she took in the solid walls, covered with tall oak bookcases, bulging with original calfskin-bound volumes.

A large fireplace to one side of the desk insulated the room from the chilly London evening, while the deep rust carpet and matching damask curtains at the tall windows secured the room against the outside world.

"Feels like home," she told him, her eyes shining with excitement.

"A sampler among all these treasures? I like that." Moving closer she said, "I always liked that poem."

Dramatically, Alistair intoned, "'Come live with me and be my love....'"

He laughed cynically. "I'm afraid most women prefer rubies to roses, and an impressive title with deep pockets to a simple shepherd with nothing but a heart to give."

"Jesus was a shepherd," Winter told him. "He sacrificed His life for love."

"That kind of love doesn't seem to go far with women these days."

Winter sensed a deep hurt inside her guardian and casti- gated herself for her quick judgments. With a compassion in her voice he could not miss, Winter said, "You've been hurt in love."

Alistair laughed, as though seeking to cover the unexpected exposure of his feelings. "It's nothing, all in the past. Why would a past love affair concern me? I'm a dashing rake, you said so yourself."

"Father always did caution me about my quick temper and even quicker judgments. I sense you are hurting." She bit her lip. "I judged too harshly, I fear. Forgive me." Reaching out, she touched his sleeve.

He melted under the plea in her soft blue eyes. Covering her hand, he cleared his throat. Why was it so easy to talk with this tiny young woman who barely reached his heart? Mayhap that was the reason. Despite the shell he constructed around his heart, she had reached him, and he didn't know how to respond.

He pulled himself up, reminding himself sharply the young woman was his ward. "Umm. Yes. From what Mrs. Duncan said, you haven't gone to services since the death of your father. Am I correct in assuming you would like to attend church?"

"Oh, yes. Is it possible?" Winter's eyes lit up, then dimmed. "Where do you usually go?"

Alistair studied his ward. The very mention of church ex- cited her, and she spoke of Jesus as though He was right there in the room with them. Scary thought. For all that, her faith drew him.

His lips twisted as his thoughts turned to the woman who had spurned him. Amelia would have scorned Winter's sim- ple but living faith.

"This will probably astound you, Winter, but I regularly worship with a small nonconformist congregation on the north side of town that adheres to the teachings of Wesley."

Winter gaped at him. "You truly worship with these people every Sunday?"

Her amazement brought forth a cold frown. "Thank you for your faith in me, Lady Renton." He relented at the lowered lashes. "I fear it is a pretty well-kept secret, so I should not be angry with you over such a trifle." The dawning respect on the face of his ward made his cravat feel decidedly tight.

"Oh, do I owe you an apology. That's all I am doing this evening, but I am sorry." She sat down with him near the hearth. "But, if I may ask, why?"

"Why the small radical congregation rather than St. George's Cathedral on Hanover Square, where the haute ton go to show off their finery?"

Winter nodded. A muscle twitched in his cheek. "It was a promise I made Mother...before she died."

"I am so glad. Here I was afraid that if we did attend services, it would be at St. George's or St. Paul's." She added, "I am sure they are lovely cathedrals and hope I can view them while I am here, but..."

Alistair nodded. "As you probably know, the ton does not go there for spiritual nourishment. Sometimes it is difficult to meditate in those churches patronized by polite society regardless of how magnificent the architecture. You'll find I am the only member of the ton to find his way to this little church I attend."

"Then mayhap," Winter said with quiet assurance, "I'll feel more at ease there."

They continued to converse for some time until a yawn seemed to catch Winter unprepared. "I shouldn't be tired already."

Taking Winter's hands, Alistair pulled her up beside him. "Just as well. I should not keep you up too late. You heard Aunt Helen. She wants to get started bright and early in the morning."

He grinned down at her. "Now off to bed with you." At her hesitation, he threatened, "Of course, I could carry you...."

"Odious man." Chin out, Winter tried to march from the room, but her leg buckled beneath her, and she fell against her guardian.

Righting her, Alistair shook his head. "I shouldn't have teased you."

"And I shouldn't be so quick to take offense. It is difficult to adjust to a guardian when I've been on my own."

The next afternoon, Winter stood in her bedchamber, shifting uncomfortably from one foot to the other to keep them from going to sleep. "Stand still," commanded the trim modiste, not for the first time.

Sighing, Winter tried to curtail her impatience by quoting Psalm 37:8, which her father had made her memorize when she was five. *Cease from anger, and forsake wrath: fret not thyself in any wise to do evil.*

She winced. Standing and turning and standing and waiting. It was hard not to fret. She was glad the modiste, thanks to the consequence of the earl and the duchess, had come to the house, instead of having to go to the woman's shop downtown.

Her mind turned toward Alistair. Why did he always seem to bring out the very worst in her?

"Lord," she muttered to herself, "help me honor him. He is my guardian. I don't understand why I get in a spin every time Justin is around."

The domineering modiste bullied her assistants and intimidated Winter, who would often have given in just to have the session over had not the duchess taken charge.

As the dressmaker and her assistants fitted and measured, held up fabrics of various styles, designs, colors and weaves, the duchess made her choices, even, at times, in the face of the modiste's suggestions to the contrary.

"No. No," the duchess said. "That color is all wrong for her. The yellow makes her look sallow."

At a particular pattern. "That bodice is much too revealing. His lordship would not approve. He wishes his ward to be stylish not provocative."

Then again. "No. No. *No!* That material is far too transparent for modesty."

Winter agreed.

"But," the woman protested, "thin fabric is all the rage."

"Absolutely not. Now put that fabric away."

Winter was horrified at all the things the duchess ordered for her. Not only did she order morning, afternoon and evening gowns, but also walking, carriage and garden dresses and more. Along with them the duchess ordered matching or contrasting reticules, hats, sashes and slippers. There were also lace nightgowns and warm robes, pelisses and capes and delicate shawls and a host of items the duchess considered necessary.

After the modiste and her assistants left, Winter sank down into the nearest chair, totally drained and out of countenance that Alistair had forced her to come to London. The cost of the gowns alone made her shiver and would make a large hole in her coffers. But to have Alistair stand the expense was unthinkable.

She would need to deal with him later when she could speak with her guardian alone. Meanwhile, she joined the duchess and Alistair in the parlour for tea wearing one of her new gowns the duchess had purchased the day before. As she entered the room, she warmed in the admiration in Alistair's eyes.

He must have noticed the lines etched under her eyes and the tenseness in her stubborn little jaw. "The afternoon tiring?"

Winter managed a nod before sitting down. She could not speak freely in front of his aunt, who had been so kind to her. Sensing her predicament the odious man smiled.

The duchess poured out the tea in dainty Dresden china cups. Cradling hers in her hands, Winter sipped gratefully, feeling the warmth flow down her throat and soothe her troubled spirit.

Later she returned to her bedchamber to rest. Staring up at the canopy over the bed she prayed. "Lord, please let her grace retire early as she did last night so I can talk to Lord Alistair."

Her prayer was not answered. After dinner the duchess joined them and stayed with them until Winter, herself, retired.

For the next couple of days, Winter scarcely saw her guardian, who always seemed to be heading out somewhere and always with a worried frown on his face. Several times she caught him in earnest conversation with Mary.

"What if she finds out?" Mary touched his arm in anything but a servile manner.

"For her sake let's hope she does not. Mary, I…"

Seeing Winter approach, Mary's hand dropped from Alistair's arm. "Ah, Winter. I was asking Mary about you." Alistair took Winter's arm. "Seems I have far too many pressing matters to attend right now to give you proper attention."

He dismissed the abigail with a nod. "But Mary tells me you are getting along fine with Aunt Helen. Even to the tutoring in etiquette. Good. Very good. Unfortunately, I must leave you again." Touching her cheek, he smiled. "Until later."

Winter watched him throw his many caped coat over his broad shoulders, place his top hat at a rakish angle on his head and stride out the door, deferentially held open by the pompous butler.

Suspicions whirled in Winter's mind. Surely her guardian wasn't seeking a dalliance with her abigail?

The only thing Winter could get from Mary was a firm declaration. "I love my husband, m'lady. Never would I do anything disloyal to him."

This left Winter puzzled and uneasy. Though she wanted to confront her guardian, she decided he was not likely to tell her the truth of the matter. Her anger simmered, believing he purposely avoided her.

Mayhap he would permit her to return home. Then she could escape being exposed to the eyes of the critical ton. She broke out in a cold sweat just thinking of her "presentation."

Her prayers became more earnest. "Why must I go through this? Please let me go home, Lord. I have no business trying to pass myself off as some refined lady."

When she cautiously broached the subject with the duchess, her grace assured Winter, "Stuff and feathers, child. Lord Alistair is planning to escort you to a social affair this very evening. Did I not tell you?"

After a bath, Mary fastened Winter into one of her new gowns. Sheer lace shimmered over the cool silk undergown. The neckline fell modestly while the sleeves puffed at the shoulders then buttoned tightly to her delicate wrists. A wide black sash encircled her high-waisted gown and a silver fili-greed band circled her head.

"M'lady," Mary exclaimed, her face alight, "you look like shimmering moonlight."

Winter smiled at the enthusiasm of her abigail, but gave it little credence until she witnessed the startled look on Alistair's face when she descended the stairs. While others might have descended slowly for effect, Winter did so because she was terrified not only of the evening ahead, but also of tripping on her short train.

Stepping down the last step, Winter, elated by Alistair's re-sponse, grinned up at him. She posed. "Do I pass your scru-tiny, m'lord?"

Frowning, he tucked her small hand in the crook of his arm. "You are much too impertinent for my ward. You are all the crack."

The duchess winced. "Justin, your cant language."

Winter frowned. "That is all right. I well know how short I fall."

His grip on her arm tightened. "Forgive me, Winter. You are a lovely young woman and don't forget that."

In the dim light of the lantern, Alistair studied his ward, wondering why his throat constricted and his heart rate increased. With a frown he realized that, after all, some young buck might look beyond her defects to her special beauty both inside and out.

Glancing up at him, Winter clasped her gloved hands. "I'll try not to embarrass you tonight."

"What?" Her hesitancy wiped the frown from his face. "I doubt you'll ever do that. In truth, I predict your card will soon be filled with young coxcombs wanting to dance with you."

"Dance? I didn't know this was a ball. I had hoped to talk to you about that." She glanced frantically from her guardian to the duchess and back again. "I don't dance!"

The duchess stared at her. "Why ever not?" Winter seemed to cringe at her impatient tone.

She whispered, "I am afraid of falling or making a cake of myself."

Mentally Alistair kicked himself. Strange. Winter was so vital and alive, most of the time, he forgot all about her problems.

"Must I dance? Mayhap you will send me back to the house?" Alistair heard the note of relief in her voice.

"No, not that." Alistair noted the fear that sprang to her eyes. "But if it bothers you, I'll stand up for you until you feel more comfortable." He put his large hand over her clenched hands. "I'll not permit anyone to hurt or to frighten you, Winter. You have to believe that."

She took a deep breath as though to steady her trembling. "I'll hold you to that."

A hush pervaded the huge, opulently decorated ballroom

when the majordomo announced, "The Duchess Ramsdale. The Earl of Alistair and Lady Renton."

Winter clutched Alistair's arm and walked without a telltale limp. Guests turned and heads bent to whisper over the silver-gowned young woman on Alistair's arm. He murmured, "I'm sensing envy."

Winter glanced toward her escort. "Who wouldn't envy me when my escort looks so refined in his black superfine formal wear."

Catching her scrutiny, Alistair whispered, "Well, do I pass muster?"

A flush burned across her cheeks. "At least no one will pay much attention to me when I am with you."

He heard her relief and was determined to show her how elegant, lovely and absolutely desirable she truly was. Desirable? For a moment he frowned. Now where did that thought come from? Surveying his companion, he once more felt his heartbeat quicken.

They followed the duchess, who introduced Winter to a host of ladies sitting in comfortable chairs set along the wall. At each, Winter smiled and did the pretty, reluctantly offering her hand even though she wore silvery gloves that disguised the deformity of her fingers.

Sitting down in one of the chairs by her friends, the duchess motioned toward Alistair and Winter. "Now, Justin, take good care of our Winter. Be sure to bring her to me if you go off."

A laconic smile touched Alistair's lips. "I know how to behave in polite company, Aunt Helen."

Nodding toward his ward, he chuckled. "You heard the duchess, Winter. You must have a good time."

With an amused grin, he led Winter onto the polished dance floor, where couples partnered in the slow, stately dance. Holding Winter closer than regulations dictated, Alistair led her into the movements. Observing the firm set of her lips, the frown of concentration in her eyes, he whispered, "Relax. I will not let you fall. Should you trip, I will hold you up and no one will ever know. Besides—" he glanced toward the other couples "—the others are too busy to notice us."

Winter murmured, "Just like Jesus."

Startled, Alistair asked, "What?"

"Like you, Jesus promised to hold us up and not let us fall. I thought He had failed me to make me come here tonight, but now—" she smiled a soft, devastating smile before continuing "—I know He sent you."

Her trust set him back. "Oh, Winter. I am far from a saint. I…"

"I am well aware of that." He wondered at the sudden flash of anger in her eyes. "But tonight you are an answer to my prayers."

Humbled, Alistair held her more securely. "Then relax. Listen to the music and move with it."

Closing her eyes, Winter seemed to let the music flow over her. Holding her close, Alistair looked down into her beautiful face, which reflected a sense of contentment and joy. He could hardly look away.

When the piece ended, she opened her eyes. "Is it over already?"

Alistair chuckled and began leading her to the sidelines when the orchestra struck up a tune and the line formed for a country dance.

A young dandy bowed before them, his neck points so high as to prevent the young man from turning his head.

"Lord Alistair, may I be presented to this lovely young woman?"

"Lady Renton, Lord Montgomery. Lord Montgomery, my ward Lady Renton."

"Your ward? Some men have all the luck." A tight smile stretched his thin mouth. "Lady Renton, would you honor me with this dance?"

Reading the panic in her face, Alistair smoothly excused

her. "Not this time, Montgomery. Winter is new in town and this is her first outing. I have promised to be her sole escort for the evening."

The young dandy raised his quizzing glass to look at Winter. "Unusual that. Quite unusual."

Winter managed to hold back her giggles at the studied actions of Montgomery. "Mayhap another evening," she told him, hoping to mitigate his disappointment, "but I am thirsty."

He bowed. "Then let me bring you something to quench your thirst."

"I would like that."

With Montgomery wending his way to the supper room, her guardian, with a frown for "Montgomery's presumption," led her back onto the floor. A new excitement swirled inside Winter. The admiration in the young lord's eyes was a heady experience.

When she was once more seated, Montgomery puffed up to them, glass in hand. "My apologies. I was detained."

Thanking him prettily, Winter took the glass he produced with a flourish. "Now, m'lady. If you will not do me the honor of standing up with me, others await."

Alistair all but snapped, "Mayhap you would have preferred dancing with Lord Montgomery. I understand he is a good catch."

Winter clutched the glass in her hand. "No. You promised."

Her answer forced the anger from Alistair's eyes. "I but jest."

Winter relaxed. "Thank you, Lord Alistair."

"Alistair, dear." At the seductive tone addressed toward her guardian, Winter glanced up only to meet the eyes of the loveliest woman she had ever seen. Taking Alistair's arm possessively, the woman pouted. "Time you dance with me, Justin. No one does this movement like you and I...together."

Irritated, Alistair disentangled his arm. "Lady Bridget. Your manners are to let."

He turned from her to his ward. "Lady Renton, Lady Bridget Trinadun. Lady Bridget, my ward Lady Renton."

"Lady Renton," the woman acknowledged. Winter shivered under the chill in her eyes.

"Lady Bridget."

Bridget turned toward Alistair. "Come, Alistair."

"I must stay with my ward, Bridget, as you well know."

"Surely your precious ward can manage a few moments without you by her side."

Alistair hesitated. "I suppose I could take you to Aunt Helen."

Bridget tugged on his arm. "She is right over there, Alistair. Surely the child is safe enough where she is until you return to her side."

Believing herself to be a hindrance, Winter also encouraged her guardian to leave her. She could not interpret the look he threw her as he allowed the gorgeous woman to lead him onto the floor.

Watching him, she could not help but admire his commanding presence. From the looks thrown his way, she realized she wasn't the only one who admired her escort. Even among the haute ton, his elegance and bearing stood out.

Later as he made his way back to her, several gentlemen stopped him and turned him aside. Her heart sank. It would probably be some time before Alistair returned.

A quiet gasp on her right drew her attention as a young woman stumbled back from the angry face of her companion. The peer turned heel and strode away from the young lady, who desperately tried to compose herself.

In a decided daze, the young lady moved toward the settee. "He wouldn't even return me to my cousin," she murmured. Covering her face, the sweet-faced young woman tried to hide her tears.

Winter said, "I am sorry you and your young man had a falling out."

Startled, the young woman stared at Winter. "He is not my young man. He…he's a horrible person."

"What did he do?"

Seeing the compassion on Winter's face, the young woman sucked in a breath. "I thought…I thought being an orphan with no portion would not matter, but it does." She gulped. "Oh, I can't tell you what he wanted." Something in Winter's gaze drew out the truth of the matter. "I thought he wanted to marry me, but he only wanted… He laughed at me. Said I wasn't worth more to him than… Mayhap I should have done what he asked. At least I would no longer be a burden to my cousins."

Winter's lips tightened with fury. "Don't judge yourself by that man's perverted values. It is that man who has a problem, not you."

The girl's eyes widened. "Truly?"

"Of course, and don't you think otherwise." Winter smiled and handed the girl a kerchief.

Wiping her face, the girl told her. "He said I would never find a man who would give me his hand. Said I wasn't worth more. By the by, my name is Millissa Wilke."

Derik's arrogant features flashed in Winter's mind, and her expression hardened. *Lord, please let me help Miss Wilke in some way.*

"I am Lady Winter Renton. Glad to make your acquaintance."

Seeing her guardian wending his determined way toward her, an idea formed in her mind.

"Lord Alistair," Winter said when he stood before them, "may I make you acquainted with Miss Wilke. Miss Wilke, my guardian, Lord Alistair."

With a tremulous smile, the young lady put out a trembling hand. Her eyes widened as Alistair elegantly bowed over it. "Miss Wilke. At your service."

Winter nodded. "That is what I wished to speak with you about, m'lord."

"Another turn about the floor," he asked as though relishing the thought of holding her in his arms.

When he reached for her hand, Winter shook her head. "You mistake the case, m'lord." She smiled a deliberately guileless smile. "I thought you might ask her."

The other young woman blushed in confusion. "M'lady. I couldn't."

With a look at his ward that promised retribution later, Lord Alistair took the girl's hand and drew her to her feet. "Miss Wilke, would you do me the honor? Then I shall restore you to your chaperone."

With only a twinge of jealousy, Winter watched the couple meet and part in the current dance.

"Want to tell me what that was all about?" he asked after restoring the girl back to her guardian. Before he returned, the girl was back on the floor with Lord Montgomery, smiling happily.

"I hope you won't be angry with me, Justin, but..." She related what had occurred. "I knew if you showed her consideration, others would flock to her side. Surely someone out there can see her for who she is and not just her lack of portion."

Lord Alistair frowned. "I can scarcely credit a gentleman would act in such a fashion toward an innocent young woman."

"It happened. I didn't hear the exact words, but I did see the way he treated her. I had to do something."

Gently, Alistair squeezed her hand. "You're pretty special yourself, Winter."

She carried the sincerity of his words and the warmth of his eyes with her the rest of the evening.

Chapter 6

"Justin," admonished the duchess in the carriage on the return trip to Alistair House. "You smothered your ward this evening." After a pause she added, "Your protection is admirable, but you scared off any contenders for Winter's hand."

Lord Alistair offered no apology. "Since she is my ward, I have every intention of seeing to it she is not hassled by undesirables."

"Doing this guardianship up a bit brown, aren't you?" The duchess cleared her throat with a certain satisfaction. "Her inheritance and natural charm will go a long way toward overcoming her...ah, problems. However, if you want to provide Winter an opportunity to make a suitable match, you must allow eligible parties access."

Winter shuddered. "If all I wanted to do was to make a good match I could have stayed home and accepted Viscount Derik's proposal. Even in London, I believe Anthony would be considered a good match. He has land and an old title. He has certainly pressed his suit hard enough. Isn't this so, Lord Alistair?"

Her guardian curtly acknowledged the truth of the matter. "Then, child, what brings you to London?"

The two women stared at Alistair, who glared back. "I thought it high time my ward at least had the benefit of a season. Besides, she needed to get away from that encroaching toad, Viscount Derik."

The duchess sniffed. "I thought he was an eligible party?"

"He is," Winter said, "but I don't like overbearing tyrants and I refused him."

The tense atmosphere prevailed all the way back to Berkeley Square. Alistair's face remained stern as he handed Winter from the carriage.

Winter's tone was soft, anxious. "I am sorry if I angered you."

Alistair gently touched her cheek. "How hard I must be on you. So many times those eyes seem tired and worried whenever you and I wrangle."

Winter closed her eyes at his light touch that warmed her clear to her toes. She was glad when he dropped his hand and took her arm to lead her inside. Stifling a yawn, Winter tried to mitigate her limp, but only succeeded in tripping.

Without a word, he carried her inside and up to her room. With a sigh, Winter leaned her head against the security of his shoulder.

He set her on her feet at the door of her bedchamber and turned her over to her abigail. "Get some sleep, Winter. Tonight was only the beginning for you."

Despite her exhaustion and before he closed the door, Winter caught the quick enigmatic glance between her guardian and Mary.

A moment later, Mary opened the door to his knock and he looked in. "Get your rest, because on the morrow I have a surprise for you."

After Mary left her for the night, and, despite the lateness of the hour, Winter read her bible for a while before snuggling under her warm covers. "Lord, thank You for a good evening and thank You that I was able to help Miss Wilke. What I don't understand is Lord Alistair. Why are he and Mary on such good terms? Why am I jealous? Lord, help him find You."

No answer came and soon her eyes closed in sleep.

The next morning Winter awoke to a bright sunny day. Her flagging spirits whisked away with her exhaustion. After breakfasting in her room, Winter let Mary help her into her new habit, a long black skirt and formfitting jacket over a ruffled white shirt. "Why the habit, Mary?"

Mary's eyes sparkled with secrecy. "Orders from his lordship." She said nothing more until she brushed out Winter's tangled hair and put it up under the tri-cornered hat.

"His lordship asked you to go on outside." James held open the solid wide door.

"Oh," she exclaimed.

At the foot of the steps, Jupiter moved restlessly next to Alistair's roan, both held by the sure confident hands of a groom with gray-blue eyes. She pursed her lips in puzzlement at his strange yet familiar eyes.

Appearing at her side, Alistair grinned. "Well?"

Her eyes shone with excitement. "I love your surprise."

"Good." He handed her onto her sidesaddle and arranged her skirt.

As she gathered the reins, she overheard the groom murmur to her guardian and watched Alistair's expression harden. "I'll be seeing the secretary of state for war this afternoon," he told the groom before dismissing him.

The secretary of state for war? What did her guardian need to see him about, and why would he tell the groom? The questions whirled in Winter's mind, but she had no time to sort out the puzzle as Alistair swung onto his roan and led the way onto the street.

In the early hour, at least for Londoners, the streets were not overly crowded. Still the street-hawkers cried their wares. Soot-covered chimney boys hurried to keep up with their employer-owners.

"Jupiter needs a hard run," Winter said. "Is there someplace we can let them out?"

Alistair shook his head at the dancing horse. "I fear London is not the place for racing. Have to make do with a long slow workout and mayhap a short canter."

For a time they rode along in companionable silence. Along their path, Alistair pointed out a London landmark here, a famous building or personage there. Winter's enthusiasm seemed to encourage her guardian.

Inside Winter bubbled. *Thank You, Lord. Thank You for this beautiful day.*

Mayhap her joy came from the unfurling leaves, the scent of flowers from some of the gardens they passed, the sun shining through the haze, or mayhap it came from the presence of the man who rode so attentively beside her.

Turning down another street, Winter exclaimed over a charming house built like a miniature castle. "What a delightful house!"

She didn't see the darkening of Alistair's expression before he growled, "I suppose you'd like me to buy it for you."

The sudden change of his demeanor shook her. "What have I done that is so dreadful? I merely admired the beauty of that house." Her bewilderment escalated to anger. "What did I do *this time* to make you so angry?"

Alistair started at the question, the muscle in his left cheek twitching. "You like the house. Were you not setting me up so you could have me buy it for you?"

Winter looked at him as though he had taken leave of his senses. "Have you run mad?"

Winter's eyes flashed, her chin jutted. Alistair sucked in a breath as though realizing, too late, his mistake. "Winter, look. I..."

He was speaking to the air for Winter wheeled her restless animal and urged him into a gallop. Her mind drummed in time with the four-footed beat of Jupiter's hooves. "Odious man. Odious man! *Odious man!*" Guardian or not, she was going home, home to the safety of people who not only cared about her, but also were wholly sane.

Paying little heed to the growing congestion of the streets, she didn't hear the clatter of hooves, the curses from the coachman, the yipping of dogs. A high perch phaeton narrowly missed her, causing Jupiter to shy. Only then did Winter begin to comprehend her danger.

The Corinthian's dalmatians nipped at Jupiter's heels. His eyes rolled white, his sides heaved from exertion. Surging forward, Jupiter ripped the reins from Winter's hands. The reins, flapping around him, increased the horse's blind panic.

Tears stung Winter's eyes and her knuckles whitened as she tangled her fingers in the horse's mane. "Lord, help me. Help! I'm sorry I let my temper get away from me again. Please don't let Jupiter be hurt, please!"

Horrified, Alistair swung the roan on his haunches and galloped after the smaller racehorse. Galloping alongside, he managed to grab Jupiter's bridle and pull the horse to a stop under a long line of trees beside a park.

"That was the most addle-pated, caper-witted thing I've seen done in my entire life! Trying to get yourself killed? I thought you cared more for your horse than that!"

Trying to calm herself, Winter sucked in several painful breaths. "Of course I do! So thank you for the rescue!" She knew she did not sound grateful, but she found his scold more than she could bear.

They cooled the horses, walking them slowly toward the town house. Neither spoke. Finally, Alistair broke the tense silence. "What did you know about that house that so interested you?"

Winter's face flushed with anger. "After your first response when I asked about it, I'd be ready for Bedlam to fall into that one."

"I really wish to know."

"I liked it, all right? But don't worry, I certainly won't ask you about anything else."

"Then you truly do not know?" Alistair said, almost to himself.

Winter found her anger fading. "Why should I know anything about that particular house? I'm hardly acquainted with London."

Alistair cleared his throat. "I, ah, bought that house for Amelia."

Winter searched her memory. Then she knew. "She was your…"

Alistair mocked himself. "I thought we had something special, but she only wanted me for what I could offer her." His glance toward Winter was contrite. "When you asked about the house…I know it was cork-brained of me, but I thought you were hinting I buy it for you."

Her temper flared. "May I remind you, Lord Alistair, you brought me to London. I have no intention of sitting in your pockets. As for all those fripperies that have been ordered for me, consider them paid for out of my accounts."

She gripped the reins. "I am sorry you were hurt by a woman of Amelia's stamp, but I am not Amelia. I don't want your fine houses, your jewels, or your money. What I want is to return to Renton Hall."

Alistair contemplated his flushed ward. "You are less than impressed with London, aren't you?"

Winter bit her lip. "Oh, I rather enjoyed my first ball last night, and I enjoy conversing with you, when you aren't up in the boughs about one thing or another. However, I do not enjoy throwing money away, and I refuse to parade like some mare up for sale at Tattersalls. I dislike being idle and feeling useless. London seems so, so frivolous." Her own inadequacies fueled her impassioned speech.

Alistair chuckled. "Not for you the position of genteel social butterfly?"

"I prefer to do something more worthwhile with my time than flit from social event to event." She felt drained. "God has given me so much, I want to give back to Him what I can. Sometimes that doesn't seem very much, but I try to…"

"Earn your way, so to speak."

"Not at all. No one can earn their way to heaven. I simply try to follow Jesus."

She sensed Alistair gaze at her serious profile. "A lot of gentlemen believe a woman's beauty is enough and that her place is gracing his table."

Winter snorted. "I'll never fit that mold. I believe God expects each of us, women as well as men, to use all the talents He has given us—and that includes our minds."

"Why do we always end up disagreeing with each other, Winter?" Alistair responded to her earnest outburst. "I know what I did was unpardonable this afternoon, but riding off like you did…." Winter read his concern.

"I, too, need to ask forgiveness." She sighed. "I keep trying to rein in my temper, but I am worse than Jupiter when he's panicked beyond reason. I just fly away, but I meant what I said. I do wish to go home."

"To Renton Hall." Alistair's lips tightened. "In a word, no. You are here. You have the chance at a season. Surely you don't want the duchess to feel she put herself out for naught. Has she not already ordered your gown for your court presentation? Besides, I think your anger is, in part, an attempt to cover up your fear that others won't accept you."

Winter wrinkled her nose. "I am going to make a cake of

myself, I just know I will. A court presentation is a dreadful ordeal."

"Mayhap, but you're scheduled to be presented nonetheless."

Again Winter sighed. "Then might I return home?"

"There is your coming-out ball."

"It just goes on and on and on."

Alistair merely smiled. "Tomorrow I take you to services."

By the time they arrived back at Alistair House, the tension had been broken, but Winter felt drained and discouraged. Some witness she was, always wrangling with her guardian. Though she hadn't openly admitted it, he was right about her feelings of inadequacy.

After luncheon, she rested and did not see Alistair leave the house in his phaeton. With seeming indifference, he sauntered into White's and found the secretary of state for war, who sat quietly reading a newspaper before an immense hearth.

Nodding to the seated man, Alistair sat in a nearby cushioned chair. For a time they chatted, ordered drinks. Both sipped absently. From a distance, it appeared the two were merely acquaintances engaged in incidental conversation. Lookers on would have been surprised at the intensity of the actual discussion.

"How long do we have?" This from Alistair.

"A week or less. Our government is getting restless, and Boney is secretly rebuilding his forces. I am thankful for what you have already done in getting our citizens back to our shores." The man shook his head. "But we have far too many who will be liabilities when it all falls apart."

"Surely Boney will let our people return home. France is, after all, a civilized country."

"Was, before that Corsican took over. Now our sources warn us that Boney might well close his borders."

"Seek revenge by seizing innocent travelers?" Alistair

swirled the dark liquid in his glass. "So you think he will invade England?"

"He's going to try. We need more information. That's where you come in."

"I'll send the *Arabella* out again tonight."

Shaking hands, the two men exchanged a look of perfect understanding before parting. Determination in his eyes, Alistair left the club. He had some serious business to attend before returning to the house.

Sunday morning dawned bright and clear. The anticipation of attending services excited Winter. She fidgeted as Mary helped her into one of her own simple muslin gowns. From what Alistair had told her, Winter decided the less pretentious gown might be more appropriate for the setting.

She was rewarded by her guardian's approval. "Good. Very good. You are a lady of rare sensibilities, my dear."

His endearment made her palms sweat beneath her gloved hands, but she managed to tease. "Mayhap I just wished to be comfortable." She smiled to ease the challenge of her words.

"I hope you do feel comfortable at these services. Puts me in mind of our small village church at my primary seat." Taking her arm, he led her from the house and handed her into the waiting landau.

He sat down beside her and waited until the coachman guided the vehicle safely onto the street. "I do believe you are as excited about attending church as you were about going to the ball."

"More so. I've been feeling starved for fellowship with other believers." Her tone was soft and sincere. "I will probably feel more at home at church than in a fancy London establishment."

She did. The building housing the congregation was small, square and hardly distinguishable from the squat, square buildings around it. The inside was austerely furnished with hard, backless benches.

The service had already begun when Alistair, his arm guiding Winter, slipped through the door and settled on a back bench. Other than a nod or two acknowledging their presence, few took notice of the late arrivals.

A well-modulated voice filled the sanctuary. Closing her eyes, Winter drank in the powerful words of the song.

Christ the Lord is risen today. Alleluia.

Surreptitiously Alistair watched his ward. Serenity and joy shone from her face in a way that made him realize such peace radiated from deep within her. He watched her listen intently to the forceful message that followed the spirited singing.

He could see this was more than a passing experience for Winter. This religion—no, *faith*—was the very core of her being. Why hadn't he seen it before? She had a center and a peace that came not from rusticating in the country, not from lack of contact with the outside world, but from her deep, personal faith.

For the first time since he was a lad in leading strings, Alistair wished for the same reality in his own faith, what there was of it.

Chapter 7

Winter descended the stairs dressed for the evening in a blue silk gown with antique lace inserts. Alistair's silk formal jacket over the de rigueur knee breeches was almost the same shade of blue as her gown. At Winter's inquiring gaze, Alistair chuckled. "Aunt Helen mentioned you were in blue tonight."

"At least this gown is simpler than that heavy court dress I wore to my official court presentation." Winter grimaced as she recalled the previous day with the long wait, the elaborate gown worn with hoops and the suffocating rooms of the official court. "I am glad that's over."

Alistair's lips twisted. "It's on to Almack's tonight, where only the crème de la crème are allowed."

"Now stop discouraging Winter, Alistair," the duchess scolded. "You well know getting vouchers for Almack's is not easy."

"The famed marriage mart." Alistair rolled his eyes as Winter stifled a giggle.

His aunt frowned at her nephew. "It is an honor."

"Hmm" was all Alistair answered, taking Winter's arm.

Inside the famed assembly rooms on King Street, St. James, the duchess greeted the patronesses who presided over the exclusive assembly rooms. With aplomb she introduced Winter, who held her breath and curtsied as the duchess had instructed her. As at the court presentation, Winter prayed her leg would not fail her.

She sighed with relief when her guardian was free to escort her onto the floor, and she relaxed at his adroit ability to hold her during the dance. Afterward, he drew her toward a group of gentlemen conversing quietly to one side.

Amusement simmered in his eyes as he introduced Winter. "My ward, Lady Renton."

A tall nervous peer bowed. "Lord Sear at your service, m'lady."

After prettily acknowledging the introduction, Winter encountered the searching gaze of a short, balding gentleman at his side.

"Lady Renton, may I make you acquainted with Lord Heywood."

Though his nod acknowledged her, his gaze was for Alistair. "Most unique, Lord Alistair. Most unique."

He smiled then at her. "Most lovely, my dear. Quite lovely, but I understand you have more in that mind than feathers."

"Of a certain," Alistair bragged. "Knows about crop rotation, and she reads more than Mrs. Radcliff."

His teasing grin widened. "In truth, I brought her to get the bronze of a town season, but she has made it clear she is not the least interested in making an advantageous match."

"Is this possible?" She felt like an insect under Heywood's quizzing glass.

"I've already turned down Lord Derik." Winter fought her rapidly rising temper.

Over the soft music, Winter heard Lord Heywood's mutter, "Alistair. A most unique entry indeed. No doubt about it, you have won the wager."

Winter's questioning glance made Alistair grimace. Placing a hand firmly on Winter's waist, he swept her into the dance and said, "I'll explain later. Promise."

With reluctance Winter nodded. As the music swelled inside her, her eyes locked with Alistair's. Suddenly no one existed but the two of them.

As the music ended, Alistair smiled into Winter's slightly dazed eyes. "I believe others are staring. Shall we?" Offering his arm, he led Winter to the side.

Alistair found a vacant chair for her, and he let her sit while he stood next to her. Nearby, the duchess chatted with her friends.

Winter smiled up at her guardian only to follow his gaze to the luscious redhead determinedly making her way across the room toward them. Her smile faded as the excitement of the evening drained away.

Lady Bridget placed a possessive arm on Alistair's sleeve. "Come, Alistair."

Winter watched him hesitate and thought he was going to refuse her. Instead, he glanced over toward his aunt. "Winter, let me take you to Aunt Helen."

"I am fine right here, Lord Alistair," she told him, her tone firm. "She knows I am here."

He hesitated. "Not quite the thing."

"Oh, just go," she told him. But when he led Lady Bridget onto the floor, the room seemed bereft of warmth.

A boisterous voice interrupted her dismal thoughts. "Lady Renton, is it not? Been deserted by your guardian already?"

Winter glanced up into the sanguine face of a blond gentleman whose exquisitely tailored jacket fit without a wrinkle over his large shoulders. Bowing over her hand, he introduced himself. "Since no one is about to do the honors, I'll do them myself. Charles Ainsworth, Lord Hollingsworth, at your service." He glanced toward Alistair and his partner. "Has he told you they have an understanding?"

"I…" Winter glanced over toward the duchess for direction, but she was deep in conversation. Winter wished she had let Alistair take her to his aunt. She stared into the overbright eyes of the man facing her. "I know you." Her eyes narrowed. "You're that rakeshame who propositioned my friend Miss Wilke."

He waved that aside. "Merely a misunderstanding," he told her. "Now you are ravishing, Lady Renton. Between us there must be no misunderstanding."

Winter leaned away from impossible flattery. "I think you should wait until we are properly introduced."

"Where did Lord Alistair find a lovely chit like yourself?"

"He is my guardian," she told him.

"You are not yet promised, I take it."

Winter laughed. "No, despite Lord Derik, no."

Hollingsworth started. "Anthony? You know him well?" His question was too casual, too emotionless.

"Our land marches side by side. Do you know him?"

Hollingsworth attempted a languid pose. "Slight acquaintances. But, if he does not hold your heart, mayhap there is a chance for me."

Winter's eyes flashed. "You probably say such nonsense to every girl you meet."

"Hardly." His tone soothed. "I am not interested in some simpering miss, but in a bright, intelligent woman like yourself."

She could not help a flush of pleasure at feeling desirable, then recalled with whom she spoke. "Lord Hollingsworth."

"Will you do me the honor?" He indicated the dance floor.

"I think not, Lord Hollingsworth."

"Charles."

She withdrew uneasily from his familiar manner. Her smile of relief seemed to dazzle Alistair as he made his way back to her. Winter noted it had not been easy to disentangle himself from Bridget's possessiveness, but he managed. Winter guessed he hurried to rescue her from the bounder hovering over her.

Lord Hollingsworth straightened, smoothing an imaginary wrinkle from his jacket. "Lord Alistair. I hear you've introduced quite a prize."

"I see you have introduced yourself." He impaled Hollingsworth with his penetrating gaze. "Lady Renton is under my protection, Hollingsworth. I trust you will remember that."

That gentleman bowed in an insolent manner. With an intimate wink at Winter he said, "Dearest Winter, I shall leave you to your oh-so-proper guardian."

"Why did you speak with him?" Alistair snapped. "Or don't you remember he is the bounder who made such an indelicate proposal to Miss Wilke?"

Winter met her guardian's carefully controlled rage with flashing eyes. "I remember quite well, thank you, but I had little choice. He refused to wait for a formal introduction and was outrageously flattering. I did nothing wrong, so why are you so angry with me?"

Winter could tell Alistair controlled his anger with some difficulty. "I am not angry with you, but I do forbid you to have any more to do with that bounder."

"Why? You can't be jealous." Winter wasn't sure why she persisted. Mayhap her own jealousy was showing? Surely not!

"Of course not." Alistair spoke with such vehemence Winter felt her cheeks pale. The evening lost its luster, and she was relieved when they returned to Alistair House. In truth, she never wished to go anywhere with her odious guardian again.

Winter headed for the stairs, her head aching almost as much as her heart, when Alistair stopped her. "I wish to speak with you, now."

The duchess had already gone up to her room, and Winter had every intention of doing the same. Throwing back her head, Winter grasped the banister and continued on up the stairs. She felt Alistair's eyes boring into her back, but refused to turn. Had she looked back she would have been surprised at the expression on his face.

Alistair turned at a knock on the door. James opened it to admit the secretary's clerk, Viscount Melton, a young peer who introduced himself. Concern etched his face. "There you are, m'lord. His lordship is calling a meeting now. It's happened. The Treaty of Amiens is all but broken, and Boney is starting to blockade his borders. Our people can't get out."

Throwing on his coat, Alistair hurried after the young man.

Upstairs, Winter's fury spilled out as Mary helped her out of her gown. "How can anyone like that man!"

"What did you do to incur his rage?" Mary spoke with deliberate calm. "His lordship isn't usually unreasonable."

"Absolutely nothing. Lord Hollingsworth introduced himself when I was sitting alone, waiting for the return of my protective guardian who danced in Lady Bridget's oh-so-willing arms. But then, they have an 'understanding' or so Hollingsworth claims.

"When Alistair saw Hollingsworth, he dismissed the man out of hand, not that I cared, mind you. I thought the man overfamiliar by half. Worse, he turned on me, as though I had encouraged Hollingsworth. He is the most—" she thought of Derik and amended "—*almost* the most odious man I have ever met."

"By morning mayhap things will not seem so bad, m'lady." Mary started to shut the door, then returned. "What Hollingsworth said about Lord Alistair and Lady Bridget…ask Lord Alistair. You might well receive a different point of view."

Unable to sleep, Winter got up, slipped on a warm robe, opened the door to her sitting room and sat down on the couch by the hearth still bright with flames. "Lord, every time I start lov—liking him, he…oh, he infuriates me." She blinked back tears. "I didn't do anything wrong, Lord. Please help him see that."

She knew the Lord would have her forgive him.

Winter closed her eyes as she wrestled with her anger. "All right. I'll forgive him, even if he doesn't deserve it."

She knew she didn't deserve God's forgiveness any more than Justin did.

Winter hung her head. "I forgive him, Jesus. Lord, forgive me, too. I don't understand why I get so angry with Justin." She paused, wondering what role the beautiful Lady Bridget really did play in his life. If there was an understanding…

For some time she considered their stormy relationship, the security she felt in his arms, the joy she felt inside when he smiled at her, touched her. She finally faced the truth of the matter as honestly as she knew how and the truth shocked her.

"Oh, no, Lord. It can't be!" she said with groan. For years she had guarded her heart, until one man, one infuriating man, penetrated her defenses. And he didn't even like her overmuch.

What was she going to do about her heart?

Much later, Alistair waited for Mary in the library. "Good, you're here. Did Terrance tell you?" Alistair rubbed his tired face. "I trust you got my ward safely tucked into bed."

"She's pretty angry with you." Mary pulled up a chair and sat down.

"I know. I have women practically fall at my feet, but not Winter. No matter what I do or say, it is the wrong thing." He shook his head. "Enough of that. We have to move quickly, Mary. His lordship said some of our most secret plans have found their way into Boney's hands. Now that we're once more gearing up for war, we have to stop that leak. Further, we have to get our people out before defense gets so tight in France we can't get through to our citizens. If we don't, who knows what will happen to them."

"Has there been a leak there, as well?"

"We're not sure, but we have to make the attempt. What about your cousin?"

"He's a gambler, but I doubt he is willing to risk his estate here for a promise of his mother's estates in France. I've never particularly cared for my cousin, as you know, but my guess is he'll try to hold on to both."

"Did Winter tell you about Hollingsworth?"

"Yes, she did. She doesn't understand why you are angry with her over the matter."

Alistair sighed and the chair creaked as he leaned back. "I'm not. But she is so innocent and so lovely. I have some explaining to do."

"If you don't want her taken in by the man, I suggest you do so as soon as possible."

She paused. "There's something else. Hollingsworth told her you and Bridget have an understanding."

Alistair groaned.

"Winter?" Alistair whispered. "Winter. There you are." He entered her sitting room on the chance she had waited up for him. From the jerk of her head and her yawn, she must have fallen asleep waiting.

Carefully he set the bedchamber candle on the stand and sat down beside her on the sofa. "Mary said you might not sleep well because of our wrangle tonight."

A distant clock struck two. "Why did you wait so long?" she asked.

Alistair hesitated. "I had to go out for a while."

"To see Lady Bridget?"

"No. In the not too distant future, we will be at war with France once more." Winter shivered. "You're safe here in London," he added.

"Is that why you insisted I come?" Winter said, "Or was it

to win some filthy wager?" He sensed her hurt. "What was it, who could present the biggest freak?"

Alistair grabbed her shoulders. "Of course not. It was to present someone of beauty and intelligence. Someone not out for a man with the deepest pockets and most elevated title. But it was more than that, Winter. I wanted to give you a season, wanted you to experience more than the day-to-day drudgery of managing your estate.

"I care about you, Winter. You are so different, alive, at peace with yourself. I envy that peace." After a pause, he chuckled. "Quite the fighter, like a little tiger."

"You were so angry tonight. I really did not like Lord Hollingsworth."

"I know. I was angry at the situation, not you."

"What did you want to see me about?" Winter lifted her face, her eyes expressive in the dim light.

"To warn you. He is not to be trusted, and, he is already spoken for." At her gasp he continued, "I don't want him to add you to his list of conquests."

"I am no fool, Justin. Why would he even look at me twice?"

Alistair smiled down at her, his heart rate quickening at her mobile mouth. "You are so lovely." His voice grew husky. "He hates me. I managed to warn away one of his potential victims, as did you. I suspect he has little love for either of us. There are other reasons as well, but we won't go into them."

"If he is a danger, why not let me return home? Surely I'd be safe there. I have been presented, and I have been to Almack's."

Putting his arms about her, Alistair held her close, felt her melt against him. "This is why, my Winter. I care. I care very much about you."

A long moment later, she pushed him away. "Justin, what about Lady Bridget. Hollingsworth said…"

He pulled back. "Winter," he said with a deep groan. "I crave your pardon. I thought only to settle things between us."

Hurriedly he got to his feet. Looking down at her, Alistair could not bear the lost look in Winter's eyes. "Winter!"

"Go," she managed to say, hugging her arms to her chest. "Go to Bridget."

"You mistake the situation, Winter. That was Hollingsworth telling a whisker. A big one."

"You and Bridget?"

"Truth? I have never encouraged her interest."

He could see she did not know how to respond. He grinned and touched her cheek. "Sleep with that thought, my dear." Picking up his chamber candle, Alistair left the room.

On his way to his own chamber he was struck with guilt. Winter was under his protection! He had no business revealing his feelings as he had. That hug, how she'd melted against him… It was almost too much to be borne. He was her guardian. He needed to remember that.

Chapter 8

The next morning, Winter decided to have breakfast in the informal dining hall only to find Alistair already filling his plate at the sideboard. After his exit the night before, Winter did not know how to face her guardian.

"Good morning. Did you sleep well?" A smile crinkled the corners of Alistair's mouth.

Blushing, she stammered, "Well enough."

From his light, impersonal conversation, the close hug of the night before might never have happened. Did his words mean so little then? Was her guardian, in truth, the rake she believed from the first?

When Winter joined him at the breakfast table Alistair felt awkward, not knowing how to respond to her. The confused hurt in her eyes when he left rather abruptly the night before cut him deeply. He had to take care how he treated her. It was almost enough to drive him to his knees. His lips twisted. Would God answer the kind of questions his heart asked? His relationship with his ward was something he wasn't ready to explore too deeply.

Alistair hurried away to visit the secretary, his mind a whirl of conflicting feelings and emotions. He did know close proximity to Winter posed a dangerous threat to his peace of mind. He was unable to forget her soft body melting into his embrace.

"Alistair." The secretary ran a hand through his thinning hair. "We have word of several of our operatives hiding in Calais."

"I'll see to it." Alistair cleared his throat. "Does anyone else know?"

"We've tried to keep it quiet, but, as you well know, there is a leak in this office, and we have yet to discover it. I'm sorry. I know this puts your people at risk."

"I'll alert the captain of my yacht. On the other hand, mayhap I'll attend to the matter myself."

"No need to put yourself in danger like that." The secretary surveyed the younger man as though sensing something amiss.

"I am going."

He shook the hand held out to him. "God go with you, Alistair."

"Yes. God," Alistair responded. Seemed at every turn he was reminded that faith mattered. Maybe it was time he considered the state of his faith. He grimaced as he considered how God viewed his lifestyle. Not so bad now that Winter had joined his household. Still and all, her deep faith made him consider the faith he once held.

For the next few days Alistair was absent without warning or explanation. In her room, Winter bowed her head. "Lord, I am so confused and angry. I want to do that which is right before You, but when Justin touches me I melt. Why did he hold me? Why did he go away?"

The next couple of days she chastised herself for her sense of desertion. She tried to hide her feelings from the too-discerning duchess, but was only partially successful. As though fearing Winter was going into decline over the unexplained absence of her nephew, the duchess tried to keep her occupied with shopping and receptions.

Winter never realized how full a day could be. At night, she blessed the duchess for the hectic schedule because her exhaustion made her fall asleep as soon as she snuggled beneath the covers.

Two verses from Proverbs 3 rang in her mind. Though she learned them many years earlier, they took on new meaning as she repeated them: *Trust in the Lord with all thine heart; and lean not unto thine own understanding. In all thy ways acknowledge Him, and He shall direct thy paths.*

Trust. She thought about the death of her father and of the accident that had disabled her and took the life of her dear mother. She demanded that God provide an explanation for what He had allowed to happen.

For the first time she began to understand that God never promised to tell her why. He asked her to trust Him. Despite everything, had He not taken care of her?

"Lord," she cried, "forgive me. I condemn Justin, but look at me. Help me to let You take care of me without always demanding to know why things happen as they do. Lord, take care of Justin, as well. I…I love him."

A smile touched her lips. As her eyes closed she mouthed the refrain.

Tiger, Tiger, burning bright
In the forests of the night,
What immortal hand or eye
Could frame thy fearful symmetry?

While Winter struggled to trust her Lord even for her relationship with her guardian, Alistair stood on the deck of his specially appointed yacht, the *Arabella*, feeling the sea spray against his enigmatic features.

In the darkness, a prayer dropped from unaccustomed lips. "Lord, protect us this night and make us successful. Lord, help me get safely back to Winter."

Under the cover of the night, the English spies boarded the *Arabella*. Only after the ship pulled away from the French coast did Alistair observe the dark shadow of a French ship pursuing them. They had been betrayed!

Alistair sent up a prayer of thanks that the French ship lacked the maneuverability of his yacht. Before dawn, the *Arabella* lay safely in the British harbour.

Later that day, the secretary, with Viscount Melton at his side, listened, unsmiling, to Alistair's report. "As soon as we make plans here, the Frenchies know it. We must find that leak or next time, you might not be so successful."

While Alistair met with the secretary, Lord Hollingsworth called at Alistair House. The duchess pressed her lips together as James showed him into the parlour.

Hollingsworth bowed to the duchess before taking a seat near Winter. "Lord Hollingsworth?"

"Charles," he protested.

"Lord Hollingsworth," repeated Winter firmly. "Why have you come to call?"

"Because I have missed seeing your lovely face."

"I've been out and about. Where have you been?"

She was surprised that he seemed at a loss, but only momentarily. "Business in the country, m'lady. Nothing to concern that pretty head of yours."

Winter started a slow burn at his condescension. "I trust you have completed it successfully."

His calculating smile chilled her blood. "Successfully enough. But I hurried back to you."

"I don't see why you are attending me when you already have a fiancée. Mayhap you were visiting her."

Hollingsworth laughed. She drew back from the intensity in his eyes. "What does my fiancée have to do with us?"

Winter's eyes widened. "What would your fiancée think if she knew you were pursuing other women?" She thought of Derik with disgust.

"You misunderstand the situation, Winter. She is a country miss. What does she know of a man's needs? I am going to marry her after all."

"What wish you with me?" Seeing the answer in his eyes, she pulled away. "Please leave." The duchess looked up, but kept quiet.

Hollingsworth captured Winter's hand. "Now, Winter, don't be a crosspatch." He lowered his voice. "Tell the dragon lady you're going to get me a book I requested from the library. I am sure I can make you understand in private."

Winter thrust out her chin. "Lord Hollingsworth, what you suggest is most improper, and you know it."

"Don't get high in the instep. I meant no harm. I do want a book."

Too late. Winter was on her feet, her hand on the bell pull. James answered her summons so quickly she suspected he waited outside.

"James, please escort Lord Hollingsworth from the house." She gave Hollingsworth no time to protest. "I will not be in to him in the future."

Hollingsworth dipped a mocking bow before exiting. Winter turned to the duchess. "Thank you, your grace. If you had not been here, I shudder to think of the liberties he might have taken. Now if you will excuse me."

She gravitated toward the library. As she entered, she found Alistair just locking a drawer in his desk.

"I am sorry if I disturbed you."

"That's all right, Winter. I only just arrived home and

planned on working here for a while before luncheon." He sat down.

Slowly she walked toward the gateleg table to pick up the book she had left lying there the day before. Book in hand, she hesitated.

Alistair glanced her way. "You will attend church with me on the morrow?"

"I'd like that."

"Something is wrong?"

Winter didn't meet his eyes. "Lord Hollingsworth was here."

Alistair's jaw tightened. "Did he make inappropriate advances?"

"The duchess was with me the entire time. He, ah, tried to get me alone in here."

At the fury in her guardian's eyes, she sputtered, "He is a dreadful man. I told James I won't receive him again."

"Glad to hear it." He took a deep breath. "Are you upset because I have been gone?"

Winter wished she could hide the color staining her cheeks. Alistair sucked in another deep breath. "I'll try not to leave you without notice again, Winter. I should have told you."

Nodding, Winter turned and left him to his work.

The next morning Alistair glanced around at the unpretentious worshippers, sitting with bowed heads all around them. Not one wore clothes as fine as those Winter wore, even though she wore one of Mrs. Duncan's loving creations.

Many wore threadbare, poor-quality garments. Many faces were lined with years of hard living. Yet those same faces held an unmistakable peace.

Alistair sensed a new, deeper peace in Winter, who sat quietly beside him. How could she be so calm when his own emotions were tangled into knots?

His shoulder brushed hers as he settled into a more comfortable position. She was so soft. With determination, he focused on the short, balding minister in a long, black frock coat whose voice reverberated throughout the small wooden structure.

The minister paced from one side of the platform. "In Christ we find purpose and peace in our lives."

His words blazed a flame thrown to the members of the congregation who sat so still, Alistair could have sworn they were all hewn from stone.

"Everyone seeks something or someone to hang on to," the minister thundered. "Each of us builds our life around something. Some build their lives around their spouse, some around their wealth, some around the lusting after fortune and fame."

As Alistair's grip on her hand tightened, Winter bowed her head. He sensed she prayed for him.

The minister alternately pounded the lectern and wiped the sweat from his forehead. "Whatever you build your life around, if it is not Christ Jesus—your life will disintegrate."

Pausing, he slowly contemplated the congregation. "You will not know peace until you accept Jesus Christ as your center, as your Lord and Savior. Only He can bring meaning and purpose into your life."

The minister thumped the lectern until it bounced. Suddenly he stopped and let silence fall, before continuing in a low voice, "Wouldn't you like to make Jesus Christ your center right now? You can. Will you come to Him today?"

Stepping down from the platform, the minister waited at the front of the building, his head bowed. Quietly, one after another among the crowd stood and slowly, reverently, moved forward. Genuine joy shone from the minister's face as he welcomed each one who stepped forward.

Alistair tensed and leaned forward. From the expression on Winter's face, he knew she expected he'd follow the others to the front. Instead, he assisted Winter to her feet and indicated his desire to leave.

Once in the carriage, he let out a long-held breath of relief.

His relief faded in the light of the disappointment in Winter's eyes. "He is your center, isn't He?"

"He is, but I am still learning to trust Him," she told him. "I wish you would also learn to trust Him."

Alistair stared beyond her out the window. "Years ago, before Mother died, I did make a decision to follow Christ." His eyes flickered to Winter's astonished face, then away. "Surprises you?"

Winter nodded, and he continued. "When she died it didn't seem to mean much any longer. I drowned my grief in the social round, but it didn't work. I guess I never did make Him the center of my life."

"You can now."

Alistair cleared his throat. The velvet of Winter's eyes made it difficult for him to concentrate. "I will think on it, Winter, my dear. I *am* thinking on it."

He knew his decision made every difference to Winter. He'd think about it…tomorrow.

Chapter 9

Winter chose a dramatic silver-over-white gown with shimmery black panels down the full sleeves and along the hem. At a time when debutantes wore either white or pastels, her gown would definitely stand out.

Surveying herself in the mirror, she knew the gown became her. Alistair caught his breath as she entered the parlour.

Her white skin glowed, as did her eyes when she found approval in his eyes. "I take it you like my choice."

"You know I do." He brought her hand to his lips.

Her eyes alight with mischief, she appraised him as he did her. Her own eyes widened at his magnificence in his black breeches and satin jacket. "Quite dashing."

Their gazes locked, and they stood together as time merged.

"Justin. Winter." The two blinked and stared at the duchess as though returning from some far place not shared by the rest of the world. Winter noticed a smile tugged at the mouth of the older woman, who must have just entered the room.

Though she glanced from Winter to Justin, she refrained from comment.

Totally in charity with one another, the two followed the duchess into the ballroom. A murmur rose from the guests and quizzing glasses snapped up at the dramatic pair. A few frowns appeared on the faces of several dowagers, but most nodded their approval of Winter's gown.

Lord Heywood motioned for them to join him. "Alistair, Lady Renton." His eyes twinkled as he perused her attire. "I am honored to pay my debt to you, Alistair. What other debutante would have the courage to wear such a spectacular and original gown?" He glanced around the room before continuing. "From the looks of it, her boldness meets with approval."

Smiling sweetly, Winter thanked him, then added, "Since, in truth, I won the wager, I believe it only fair that I get to decide where that money goes."

Alistair's eyes narrowed with cynicism. "How would my lady wish to spend my ill-gotten gains? A sapphire necklace?"

Winter's eyes flashed, letting him know he had made a mistake. "I have little need of such trifles, m'lord." Alistair flinched, before his lips turned up slightly as she continued to speak. "But I do believe there is a small, nonconformist congregation who could use the money, if they are not made aware it is tainted money."

Alistair dipped his head in acknowledgment. "Heywood, the lady is correct. She won the wager and the winnings shall be designated as she wishes." His laughter rang hollow as he gave the peer the direction of the pastor.

Drawing Winter onto the highly polished floor, he whispered, "Don't want me to keep my ill-gotten gains."

Winter stiffened in his arms. "'Twas only fair. You tricked me into coming to London. You did so with less than upright motives."

He acknowledged her rebuke with a slight bow. "My apologies. I should have known better."

"You should." They parted and came together in the slow, stately dance.

"I was only angry when I thought you were forcing me into buying fripperies for you."

As they parted he saw the flash of disappointment in her eyes. Hurt at her judgment, he held her closer than decorum dictated.

Afterward he led Winter aside. Seeing her tentatively lick her lips, an action that sent a shock through him, he asked, "Shall I get you something to quench your thirst?"

"Thank you, Lord Alistair. I would so appreciate that." She leaned against the column entwined in flowers. "If you do not mind, I'll wait for you here."

Nodding, Alistair hurried off.

A shadow blocked out the light from the chandeliers. Winter looked up into Lord Hollingsworth's taunting face. Taking her hand, he tucked it into the crook of his arm before she realized what he was about.

"Lord Hollingsworth, please desist." She tried to pull back her hand, but he held it fast.

"I want you to take a short stroll with me."

"Not now." She tried to smile.

The man's eyes narrowed. After a moment's hesitation, he spoke in a tone that sounded too smooth, too polished. "My dear Winter, Alistair has been detained." He managed to make it sound as though she well knew what had detained him.

"Lady Bridget?" Despite Alistair's assurances, Winter wondered how he could not be tempted.

"As I passed, he asked me to escort you to him. Not good for a young woman to be alone."

"If he is occupied," Winter said as the excitement of the evening faded, "take me to her grace."

"I saw her go off to the card room. I fear, my dear, you must do as Lord Alistair asks. He is your guardian after all."

"I suppose." Something warned Winter to stay put. Yet what harm could he do in the sad crush? Besides, Alistair would be in a spin if she refused his request.

She permitted Hollingsworth to lead her triumphantly across the crowded room toward the balcony opening out from the French windows. Winter balked and pulled back. "My lord, I don't believe I should leave the ballroom."

His eyes dark and smoldering, Hollingsworth grunted. "Don't be a fool. Where else would a man bring his lady friend for some privacy?"

"Are you saying Alistair is out there? I don't know...." She still held back.

"Oh, I see it now. You are afraid of Alistair. Has he already tried to take advantage of you?"

Willing herself not to blush, Winter straightened. "No, I am not afraid of my guardian. Lay on, MacDuff."

Head high, chin out, Winter walked out onto the balcony on Hollingsworth's arm.

The night air was heavy with the fragrance of a variety of spring flowers. Through the windows she heard laughter and the murmur of voices, strains of a robust country dance and out on the balcony—silence.

"Where is Alistair?" she demanded, trying to peer around Hollingsworth, who deliberately blocked her view.

As he moved out of her line of sight, Winter searched for her guardian, but no tall form came toward her.

"You lied," she insisted. "I must return immediately."

Hollingsworth blocked her exit, his hands on her arms. "Winter, listen to me. I want you."

"What about your fiancée?"

"She's in the country, and I need a woman here. Listen to me." He forced her to look at him. "I don't want to hurt you. I want to shower you with everything you could want. Diamonds? Sapphires?"

"Aren't you forgetting my guardian?" asked Winter.

"Surely we can plan our rendezvous without putting him in mind of our actions."

"Why would I want to do that? Alistair has been all that is kind."

"True, I cannot now provide for you as does your arrogant guardian so-called, but soon, soon I'll be able to provide for you beyond your wildest imaginations."

Color rose in Winter's cheeks. "So-called. What do you mean so-called? Alistair was appointed my guardian by my father."

He snorted. "I am not fooled by the presence of her grace. Alistair is your protector."

Outraged, Winter jerked away. "I, too, am a country woman like your fiancée, and I pity her for having to marry such a miserable excuse for a man."

Grabbing Winter to him, Hollingsworth bruised her soft lips with his brutal kisses. He released her only at the laughter of another couple walking toward the window.

Taking the opportunity, Winter slapped Hollingsworth soundly across the face. Picking up her skirt she limped quickly back into the room almost bumping into her furious guardian.

"Alistair, I am so glad you're here."

"Now you are glad!" He slapped a glass into her hand. "It appears you worked up quite the appetite for this." She shivered under the freeze in his eyes. "Or have you someone else awaiting your favors?"

"It isn't what it seems." Her chin jutted even while she blinked back tears. "What was I to do with you off with your flirt?"

He growled, "Have you run mad?"

For a moment they stared at each other. Winter trembled. "Please, will you take me home?"

He nodded curtly. Together they found the duchess. His face

a cold mask, Alistair ushered them into their carriage. Though she felt his gaze, Winter refused to meet Alistair's eyes.

The duchess seemed to sense something seriously amiss and kept her peace. However, before her grace stepped gracefully from the carriage, she whispered in Winter's ear, "I'm praying for him, too, my dear. Don't give up on him."

Startled, Winter stared after the woman, her mouth gaping. Trying to take in the implication of the duchess's simple statement, Winter hardly realized she was inside until Alistair released her arm.

"Good night, m'lord," she told him firmly, formally.

His lips tight, Alistair wished his aunt the same, then sprinted up the stairs. Winter followed more slowly with the duchess, who turned off to her rooms.

Her leg cramped painfully, and she clenched her teeth. Sensing her depression, Mary said little as she helped Winter into her night dress. At the door later, she turned. "Things will be better tomorrow."

Would they? Winter's heart felt like it was being ripped in two by Alistair's condemnation. She replayed the evening, wondering what she might have done to forestall what happened.

"I am such a green-goose, Lord. Why couldn't I have guessed Hollingsworth was lying?" She closed her eyes against the tears. Anger burned with hurt that her guardian would assume the worst.

"Now what, Lord? Alistair surely will never believe me again. Never believe in You. I wish I had never come to London."

Unable to sleep, Winter finally slipped from the bed and wrapped a long satin robe around her slender figure. Lighting a bedchamber candle from the still glowing embers in the hearth, she crept out into the dimly lit hallway, descended the stairway and made her way to the library.

Hoping to find a book to distract herself, Winter pushed

open the heavy door expecting to find the room dark. Standing in the doorway, she blinked rapidly in the brightly lit room, focusing on Alistair hunched over his desk.

She could not, would not, face him tonight. Taking a step backward she prepared to return to her bedchamber when Alistair glanced up. "Winter? What?"

"I couldn't sleep so thought I'd find a book to read."

"Please come in."

Winter hesitated before venturing farther into the room. She sensed he studied her guarded expression. "What happened with Hollingsworth tonight?"

She heard the accusation, more she heard a certain disappointment. How foolish she had been in believing Hollingsworth!

"Winter, come here."

Her back straight, shoulders stiff, she moved toward him, her eyes wide with unshed tears. Suddenly she stumbled, felt Alistair's strong arms grab her and lead her to the couch.

"Please tell me what happened."

"Hollingsworth said you were busy with, ah, Lady Bridget, and had asked him to escort me to where you were. I was such a goose to believe him."

Alistair covered her hand with his own. "Go on."

"When I realized he had lied, I tried to leave, but he wouldn't let me. He went on about wanting me for himself, about meeting him in secret. He said he would soon have the means to give me anything I could ever want.

"He…he kissed me. It hurt." She touched her lips as tears trickled down her cheeks. "You were so angry with me.

"I don't understand why he wants me. He doesn't want to marry me, he only wants… And Derik only wants my property. Can't anyone love me for myself?"

As though not trusting himself to speak, Alistair gazed at her searchingly before wrapping his arms around her.

"Are you like Hollingsworth? Do you want something from me, as well?"

"No!" Alistair objected. "I will not hurt you, Winter. You are a very innocent and lovely young woman, and I care about you very much."

Laying her head against him, she sighed contentedly. "I was so afraid. Afraid you hated me, afraid I had turned you away from God forever."

"Is that important?"

"Yes, because…because…" Her words trailed off.

"Because why?"

"Because I think I lo—care for you," she whispered.

"Oh, Winter." His face reflected tenderness.

When he said nothing more, Winter hid her face against him so he could not see her hurt. He cared, but not enough. Or did Lady Bridget stand between them?

"I want to go home."

"No," he growled. "You will stay. I promise not to do anything to dishonor you."

Alistair's work was only a guise to keep his thoughts at bay. Why could he not make Winter happy by committing his life to the Lord as she asked? What held him back?

She loved him. Something warmed inside him, and yet he held back. Amelia, too, had declared her love. They were not alike, these two. How could he compare Winter's openness and honesty to Amelia's deceptive wiles?

His heart stopped, started again. "Why, I love her. I do. I love Winter."

Suddenly he straightened. Hollingsworth told Winter he would soon be deep in the pockets. Was that all a hum? He was deep in dun territory, so how… He asked Winter to take him to the library? Alistair's thoughts rocked him with their implications.

Hollingsworth? He was in the Horse Guards and had friends

in the office. He came and went as he desired. Was there a more sinister connection?

Sitting there with his arms around her, Winter had fallen asleep. With a tender smile, he got up and carried her up to her room. Brushing a featherlight kiss across her cheek, he set her on her feet outside her room. As she awakened, he opened the door and pushed her inside. "Sleep well, Winter." She blinked as he gently closed the door and headed for his room. There would be precious little sleep for him tonight.

The next morning, before Winter awakened, Alistair left the house to meet with the secretary. To his surprise, a tall young peer met him in their usual spot. "Spensor Melton," the young peer said quietly. "The secretary thought your meetings were becoming too noticeable, so he sent me."

Alistair frowned. "I've seen you before…the clerk at my door and in the secretary's office." Melton nodded and handed over a letter of confirmation.

Alistair read the letter, before assessing the assured young man. Melton read the question in his eyes. "Yes, I am young, but I already lost a friend to the accursed Corsican. I offered my services, such as they are."

Melton had a firm handshake and a steady gaze that drew Alistair's trust. Alistair tucked the note into his pocket before giving his report.

Head tilted, Viscount Melton listened to Alistair's suspicions. "Does Hollingsworth have reason to be involved? I mean, he may be a bounder, but a traitor?"

"I think it is worth checking out, don't you?"

"Are you perhaps overreacting due to his overtures toward your ward?"

"I don't think so." Alistair's voice was hard. "She's hardly his type. Small of stature, not exactly the build he usually goes for. And, she, uh…she is disabled, somewhat." He spoke the last reluctantly, surprised that he scarcely thought of her limitations any longer.

"We are aware that he is engaged to some country miss." The viscount pursed his lips. "That might stand checking out."

"Her father's estate is not far from my own country seat."

"I see." Melton's gray eyes narrowed with thought. "Might you have some pressing business to take care of in the country?"

"Hmm." A laconic smile stretched Alistair's lips. "I am certain I mentioned it."

Winter awoke to a quiet house. Downstairs, she encountered the duchess. "Have you seen Justin?"

"Have the two of you discussed your differences and made things right?" The duchess actually winked, and Winter blushed.

"I think so. Where is he?"

"I am sorry, but he was in somewhat of a hurry when I saw him. Said he had some pressing business in the country. Be gone for several days as I understand it."

The happiness faded from Winter's face. "Oh. He didn't leave any messages for me."

"Not that I know of other than to tell you what he told me." Winter felt bereft. Again he had gone off without telling her as he had promised he would. Anger surfaced, then acceptance. He left because he promised not to hurt her. She could respect him for that.

Her spirits low, she decided that maybe a ride on Jupiter would raise them. Terrance Carlyle, the tall groom who seemed so familiar earlier, accompanied her. His engaging manner was not quite servile. His smile infectious. Still her flagging spirits did not revive. Later, Winter attended the opera with the duchess and a particular friend of hers, an elderly but dashing peer who made Winter feel awkward and out of place.

Winter knew it was time to face reality. Without Justin's

presence, she disliked the social round immensely. Since he had gone away without a word to her, she concluded he was trying to distance himself from her against a declaration of love.

"Poor man is probably in a state of shock," she told herself. "Still, why did he hold me like that?"

Could she dare hope he might someday reciprocate her feelings? What had she to offer beside the likes of Lady Bridget?

Trust me, came the voice inside.

"I am trying Lord, I am trying."

More and more she longed for the security of Renton Hall.

Chapter 10

Winter rode Jupiter in the early morning. Though she enjoyed the ride, the tall trees and meandering stream in the park only heightened her longing for the green fields, open countryside and clean air of Renton.

Beside her on a restless gray rode her usual escort, Terrance Carlyle. His easy manner and self-confidence gave her a sense of security. That morning, she found Mary wrapped in the groom's long arms. Seeing her averted face, Terrance Carlyle chuckled.

Mary cuffed him playfully. "Have done, Terrance."

Smiling, she addressed Winter. "Lady Renton, may I make you acquainted with my husband, Terrance Carlyle."

"Ah," he said to Mary and chuckled, "our lady thought we were engaging in a few stolen moments, my love."

Winter flushed as her eyes met the amusement in the man's eyes. Definitely not servile! She was recalling the incident and puzzling over the thought that his behavior seemed more to the manor born than the stable when Hollingsworth loomed up beside her on a huge black gelding.

"Winter, fancy meeting you here at this hour."

Winter guided her horse away from the encroaching gentleman and urged Jupiter into a canter. The groom smoothly followed, a decided smile on his face.

Hollingsworth kicked his animal into a canter. Fighting the animal, Hollingsworth caught up with Winter, who slowed Jupiter at the turn. Again, Hollingsworth hauled on the reins, seesawing them against the animal's tender mouth. Curses rolled off Hollingsworth's tongue.

Winter turned Jupiter to face him. "Stop abusing that horse!"

"I'll do what I like with what is mine," the man growled, his face red with exertion. "I've tamed wilder ones than this." Winter heard the slap of the whip on the horse's rump and winced as the animal shuddered.

A slender groom rode beside his master. Winter heard him try to calm the horse with his soothing voice. Again Hollingsworth held the reins so tightly he arched the horse's head, almost touching nose to chest. "Haven't seen Alistair of late."

Winter snapped, "He has been busy." She had her hands full trying to keep her own frisky animal still.

Hollingsworth's horse shifted and again the bounder slapped the whip. "Out chasing his bit o'muslin, mayhap?" For a second his eyes narrowed. "Has he left you all alone in the wicked city?"

"Cyprians are your department, Hollingsworth," Winter countered.

"So he warned you, did he?" The man struggled a moment, cursed, then managed a leer. "I daresay his affairs have been more touted than my own." Winter was unable to hide the hurt that flitted across her face, and Hollingsworth nodded in satisfaction.

Terrance Carlyle interjected. "M'lady, I believe it is time for us to return."

Hollingsworth noticed the tall groom for the first time. "Too familiar by half," he drawled. "Groom, is it? Mayhap the lady has been dallying with more than her erstwhile guardian."

Winter's angry flush and quick denial brought a sneer to Hollingsworth's lips.

"M'lady," Carlyle growled, "we need to go."

For a moment the black paused, heaving from his exertion. Hollingsworth took the moment to look more closely at the groom. "Strange. You bear a marked resemblance to the Stuart family. Wrong side of the blanket? Good. Quite good that." He roared with laughter.

Now Winter, too, saw the resemblance. No wonder he had seemed familiar. No denial sounded from the groom's tightly controlled expression. Winter felt his hatred of Hollingsworth as a physical thing.

Hollingsworth taunted her. "A *tendre* for Alistair, is it?" The black shook his powerful head against the choking reins.

"You blush so easily, my dear. Don't be deceived. That rogue will take your heart and your innocence far more smoothly than I, but he has no more intention of offering marriage than I have."

"So you say, but with all the other lovely widows of the *ton*—" she thought of Lady Bridget "—why would you single me out for your favors?"

Hollingsworth cursed when the black tried to sidle away from Jupiter. "Mayhap I wish to know why Alistair attends you—and he is so attentive. I see it now, a touch, a soulful look. A hug. Oh, he's smooth that one."

Winter clutched Jupiter's silky mane. Hollingsworth witnessed her response. "Ah, so he has gotten that far."

Her eyes darkened. "Justin has not hurt me in any way."

"You are an innocent. One of these days Alistair will reveal his true colors, and when he does—come to me."

"Never!" Winter lifted the reins to give her restless horse his head. It amazed her he had remained as calm as he did beside Hollingsworth's unruly mount. Then she saw Carlyle's hand on his mane and realized the groom had been keeping him quiet. She sent him a grateful smile.

Seeing what she was about to do, Hollingsworth kicked the black as the whip once more descended on his hindquarters. Neighing, the sensitive animal reared, neatly dumping the unsuspecting lord onto the hard ground. Terrance Carlyle laughed outright, while Winter's own giggle pealed forth before she could contain it.

His face hot with fury, Hollingsworth stiffly got to his feet and carefully dusted himself off. His groom, who was busily soothing the wild-eyed horse, didn't see Hollingsworth pick up his whip, nor did he see the menacing arm lifted before the whip descended on his groom's unsuspecting shoulders.

"You incompetent scoundrel," Hollingsworth roared. "This is all your fault." Hollingsworth cursed the poor groom, who tried to dodge while holding on to the struggling horse.

Screaming curses, Hollingsworth raised his whip once more, bringing it down again and again across the shoulders of both groom and horse.

"Stop it! Stop it right this second!" With a boldness born of desperation and compassion, Winter rode Jupiter between Hollingsworth and his victims.

Though he pulled his swing, he could not stop in time and the whip snapped against Winter's arm, slicing her riding jacket to the elbow. Hearing his mistress's groan, Jupiter swung about, knocking Hollingsworth to the ground.

Terrance Carlyle rode to her side. "Are you all right?" he asked, glowering at Hollingsworth, who was once more getting to his feet.

Fingering the tear, Winter nodded. Her arm stung where the whip slashed, though the skin did not appear broken.

Hollingsworth's groom and horse stood trembling nearby.

Reaching for the reins, Hollingsworth growled at the groom. "I'll see to you later."

After considerable difficulty, and with his groom holding on to the large animal, Hollingsworth managed to regain his seat. Turning, he glared into Winter's cold white face. "I hope you are satisfied, but you wait, innocent miss. One day I'll have you in my power. One day."

She retorted, "I hope I never see you again, Lord Hollingsworth." She cantered away, feeling a chill between her shoulder blades.

"You're well shot of him," said Carlyle.

She shuddered. "Thank you for your help. I am glad you were there." She managed a smile while her heart cried. *Lord, please keep that dreadful man away from me.*

His insinuations had done their damage, though. The seeds of doubt Hollingsworth planted in Winter's mind about Alistair's intentions brought back her own initial doubts.

"You mustn't mind what he said about his lordship." She realized Carlyle correctly guessed the direction of her thoughts. "His lordship is an honorable man."

"Perhaps," she said, remembering the whispered conferences and easy familiarity between her abigail, Carlyle's wife, and Alistair. She wondered anew about Amelia. Then there was that intimate hug. Her cheeks flushed.

Sooner or later Alistair would return. She believed him when he told her he would not harm her, but just what was his definition of *harm?*

How could she forget his touch? When he put his arms about her, she lost all sense of propriety. No, she was much too vulnerable to him. Only one solution presented itself—she must return home.

Against Mary's protestations, Winter insisted she pack a trunk. "Whatever doesn't fit, leave."

Mary begged, "At least wait until his lordship returns."

"No, there is no time to lose."

It was more difficult to inform the duchess of her intentions. Truth to tell, she waited until her trunk was loaded on the carriage she had ordered.

"Why didn't you tell me you had an engagement, child? Who is attending you?"

"I am sorry, your grace, but I have decided to return home where I belong."

"Haven't you been happy here? Does Alistair know of this?"

"No, and don't ask me to wait for him to return for I won't."

Winter knew the duchess recognized the futility of further argument. "You must not travel alone." After a moment of thought, her face brightened. "That's it! I'll send Mary and Terrance with you."

"No need, your grace," Winter said, but was grateful the duchess insisted.

The duchess continued, "Terrance can ride that gelding of yours home."

Less than an hour later, Winter waved to the duchess from the comfortable seat in the coach.

"I'll keep you in my prayers, child."

Blinking back her tears, Winter managed to say, "Thank you, your grace."

The coach bumped along the narrow roads, causing the passengers to sway from side to side. Winter withdrew in the corner, her thoughts already on Renton.

"I'll have to check the books," she told herself. "Have all the crops been put in, I wonder?" On and on she planned the list of activities she expected to keep her busy for some time to come.

She knew Alistair had sent over a manager, but she well knew no one could do the job with the same sense of dedication and responsibility she did. Thinking about home brought a slight smile to her lips. Home. She could hear Mutton-head's yips of welcome, feel his cold wet doggy kisses. She belonged at Renton Hall.

The day stretched long and uncomfortable in the swaying, jerking coach, and Winter was glad to stop for the night at a posting inn. The room was clean and the food presentable. The beds had been turned and did not appear to contain vermin, and yet Winter found herself unable to rest.

She felt the Lord asking her why she didn't wait on His instructions, why she didn't ask Him about going home.

"But, Lord," she argued, "what else could I do? I don't belong in London."

Tired, the next day's journey seemed to take forever. On the one hand, she ached to demand the coachman urge the grays on, on the other, she wanted to scream, "*Stop!* Return to London—and Justin—at once." She did neither.

Mary tried to divert her thoughts. "Would you tell me about Renton Hall?"

The question kept Winter reminiscing for some time. She nearly forgot about Mary until she asked, "Viscount Derik. You say you are close neighbors?"

"Neighbors, yes, but not close friends." She grimaced. "Never cared for him above half." She shook her head. "Can you believe it? He insists we would suit."

"Is that why you are going home, to accept his proposal?"

"Never!" Winter shuddered. "I will never, never marry Lord Derik!"

Though she could not be sure, she thought Mary gave a sigh of relief.

When the rambling manor house came into view, Winter announced, "Home at last! Look, Mary. This is where I belong."

For the first time since leaving London, Winter laughed.

Carlyle carefully assisted Winter to the ground before reaching up for Mary. His large hands spanned her waist, and he swung her to the ground with a flourish.

"Come on, Mary," Winter cried, barely able to contain her excitement as she led the way to the manor.

Duncan grinned at the sight of her. "Miss, m'lady. I didn't expect you."

With a giggle, Winter hugged the graying butler before stepping into the house. Hearing the commotion, Mrs. Duncan hurried toward the entryhall. "M'lady." The woman's ample arms enfolded the young woman.

Winter laughed as the housekeeper released her. "May I make you acquainted with Mary Carlyle. Mary, my housekeeper and friend and her husband, Mr. and Mrs. Duncan."

The two women surveyed one another before Mrs. Duncan inclined her head. "M'lady."

Mary glanced toward Winter, who did not appear to have noticed the housekeeper's assumption. Mrs. Duncan continued, "I thought you safely in London. His lordship said..."

"Has Lord Alistair been here recently?"

"Two days past. Said you took London by storm. Seemed right proud of you."

"Oh, Mrs. Duncan," Winter choked out, "I just want to be home."

Turning to Duncan, she said, "Please see to the coachman and grooms. They will be leaving at first light on the morrow. Mary, too."

She faced the housekeeper. "You will show Mary to her room. Oh, and, Duncan, have my trunk brought in. Thanks."

With a sigh, Winter started down the hall. The long journey had cramped her leg, and she paused to rub it. Hearing a rustling of papers in her father's study, she opened the door. Hunched over the large desk was a middle-aged man with gray-peppered brown hair.

"Sir, may I ask who you are?"

Putting down his pen, the man swung around to face her. "Yes." She heard his irritation at the interruption. "Who are you, if I may ask? I am busy."

She straightened. "I am Lady Renton."

With a grunt, the man hastily got to his feet. "Forgive me, m'lady. I am Mr. Jonas, your estate manager."

Winter thought he looked both solid and reliable. "Glad to make your acquaintance, Mr. Jonas."

"You wish to go over the books, mayhap?" He cleared his throat as though the thought was untenable. "His lordship said you used to keep the books."

"Used to," Winter repeated. "Ah, yes. I did. There was no one else, you see." She stopped, wondering why she needed to defend herself. "I suppose his lordship has checked the ledgers recently."

"Matter of fact, yes."

"Two days ago."

"Yes."

"Then never mind, Mr. Jonas."

"As you wish, m'lady."

He had already returned to work by the time Winter closed the door behind her.

Why had Alistair stopped by? He knew how much she wanted to come home. Could he not have at least permitted a short visit since he himself was obviously in the neighborhood? The tangle of questions pursued her, but she tried to put them from her mind.

Closing her eyes, she drank in the familiar sights and sounds. She heard the creak, creak of the floorboards, smelled beeswax and lemon from wood recently polished, sniffed the inviting odor of venison wafting from the kitchen. Suddenly she was ravenous.

Reaching her room, she found the housekeeper already unpacking her things and exclaiming over her London creations. "Oh, miss, m'lady." Reverently the matronly woman stroked the material. "Such elegance and style. I cannot wait to see you dressed up."

"Right now, I want something more practical. I am home,

and I want to be comfortable." She began taking off her crumpled traveling suit.

Taking a simple green gown from the closet, the housekeeper settled it over Winter's head. Picking up the hairbrush, Mrs. Duncan brushed out the tangled locks. "Look at yourself in the mirror, m'lady. I'll wager even your guardian made sheep's eyes at you."

Winter attempted to hide the pain that flashed in her eyes. "Missy…" The housekeeper forgot her formality in her concern. "Your guardian, he didn't…hurt you?"

"No, nothing like that, Mrs. Duncan." She sighed. "Not that it matters. I am home now, and here I plan to stay." She forced cheerfulness. "Think dinner is ready? I am famished."

The housekeeper hesitated. "Miss, something is definitely amiss. There is a sadness about you… Something…" The thought faded at Winter's withdrawn expression.

Winter took Mr. Jonas's presence at the table as a given. She assumed he was a gentleman without prospects who had been hired by Alistair. Mary's presence, however, was a surprise.

At her startled glanced, Mary whispered, "I believe Duncan thought I was your companion, not simply your…"

Glad for the other woman's presence, Winter sat down. "So you are."

Mr. Jonas, much to his chagrin, found himself the target of Winter's astute questions. "Sounds to me like you have everything well in hand, Mr. Jonas. I commend you." Winter bestowed a smile she hoped he would not recognize as false. How could he know how displaced Winter was beginning to feel in her own home?

After dinner, Winter retired to the parlour—alone. Mr. Jonas pleaded more work and Mary went to see her husband. There was nothing for Winter to do, no one with whom to share the evening that stretched tediously before her.

Firmly she blinked back the tears that threatened to fall. "Lord, I should not have come home."

Later, she decided a walk in the garden would clear her mind. She slipped open the French doors and stepped down to the garden. The night was still and myriad stars twinkled overhead, a sharp counterpoint to the pain in Winter's heart.

She meandered along the hedge surrounding the fragrant flowers. Hearing muffled voices, Winter shrank out of sight. If it was a maid out with her beau, she would be most embarrassed to be caught out by her mistress.

Her smile faded as she identified the arrogant tones of Lord Derik and Mary's lilting voice.

"What are you doing here, Cousin Mary? Rusticating in the country, are you? Or are you with the chit?"

"Leave her alone, Anthony. I know you are trying to force her into marriage, but I assure you Lord Alistair will have none of it."

"Dear, sentimental cousin. Has working for the English softened your heart?"

"You are more English than I, Anthony. Leave her alone, she's an innocent. Why bother her anyway when you'll soon have everything you ever wanted?"

"Her upstart father wouldn't give me the time of day. Well, I have every intention of getting everything—this estate and his dear," he intoned with sarcasm, "daughter. Besides—" he paused before continuing "—I have debts to pay."

"Gambling debts, I suppose. But why now?"

"Why now? Because Boney is about to acknowledge my claim on my mother's French estates? Why not have everything? I need money for passage and to claim what is rightfully mine."

"But marriage. I cannot believe you care for the girl. You never cared for anyone but yourself."

"How true, Cousin Mary. Through her, I get Renton, and who is to care if the damsel proves too fragile for married life."

Winter heard the cruel satisfaction in his voice. "I'll leave the rest to your imagination, cousin. But since you are in this as deep as I, I have little fear you will tittle-tattle to her pompous guardian. In fact..."

"Ow! Let go of my arm."

"You will help me by praising my suit to him."

"What if I refuse?"

"I'll turn you in. They hang spies. Nasty business that."

"You can't see her tonight. I want to make sure no one sees us together."

"No, we wouldn't want that." There was a pause. Winter hugged herself to keep from shivering. "The count reports you have sent him valuable information. Good thing we discovered his lordship has access to the most secret of information. With two arteries into the government, we can use one to check the other—just in case you should betray us to that dashing employer of yours."

"Stop it, Anthony. I have no personal interest in the man."

Winter shrank farther into the garden as the conspirators bid each other good-night. Moments later, Winter edged back to the house.

She was closing the French doors when Duncan startled her by announcing, "There you are, m'lady. Would you like something to drink before retiring?"

Shivering, Winter stammered, "Hot chocolate would taste good. Thank you."

"As you wish, m'lady."

All night Winter tossed. *Trust in the Lord...let Him direct.* She hadn't done very well on that score, she decided. It was far too easy to go her own way. What had she found at the home to which she had run? Security? Hardly. She thought of Derik.

Purpose? Not with the competent Mr. Jonas in charge.

What of Mary? Alistair had been so sure Mary was not a

threat. What had she done to fool him into thinking she was not a French spy? But she was. Winter almost wished she had not found out.

Alistair would be devastated to discover Mary's ruse. Did he care for her? The thought pained Winter. Whatever Alistair was, he was a patriot. Somehow, somehow Winter knew she had to let him know the truth about her abigail…and Lord Derik.

Lord Derik. She shivered at his cold-blooded plans for her. For all that, they didn't surprise her overmuch. He had always been cold and uncaring to both people and animals.

When finally she slept, Winter dreamed of Justin's arms holding her tight. "In the morning," she told herself sleepily, "I'll send a letter back with Mary." But Mary and her husband had started back to London before she awoke.

Late the next morning, she went over the ledgers with Mr. Jonas and, as she expected, found them in order. Still trying to decide what to do about Mary, Winter changed into a dark blue wool riding habit and boots. A stable boy helped her onto the restless gelding while Mutton-head barked and barked, wriggling every inch of his small dark body.

Turning away from the manor hall, Winter rode to visit her tenant farmers. They greeted her with enthusiasm.

"Lady Renton, good ta see ya. Thought ye be a-takin' London over," called a grizzled farmer, rubbing his bearded face.

Winter sounded a false laugh. "I missed you all."

"Aye, lass, the land's in yer blood, sure enough. And glad yer back, I am."

"How is Mr. Jonas?"

"Good man, he is. Already showed us how to get more out of the farm."

"Glad to hear it," Winter said, not at all truthfully, before riding on. Wherever she went the next few days the message was the same. Mr. Jonas was not just as good a manager as she, he was clearly better.

Galloping the horse up to Renton Hill, Winter stared over her estate…and wept.

Chapter 11

When Winter returned from her ride, she was dismayed to find Viscount Derik awaiting her in the east parlour. Reluctantly she entered, refusing the housekeeper's suggestion that she change out of her dusty habit.

If the viscount persisted in his proposals, she was not going to encourage him in any way. However, from Derik's speculative perusal, she could tell he appreciated her fitted habit that showed her soft curves to advantage. His survey made her wish she'd changed into something a bit more shapeless.

"Winter." He bowed without taking her hand. "I was glad to hear you had returned home." A sardonic smile lurked at the corners of his mouth. "Tired of the unwanted attentions of some St. James dandy, or was your erstwhile guardian tired of dancing attention? You are not promised, I trust." He made it sound as though the thought was ludicrous.

"No, as you well know."

"I see." A predatory light shown in Lord Derik's eyes. "How was I to know you were not promised?"

"Because you don't believe anyone would want me." She heaved a silent sigh of relief she had not given away that she overheard him and Mary in the garden.

"Were you asked," he asked with a leer, "to fill another role, mayhap?"

Winter felt a chill start down her back. "You seem to know an awful lot of what happened in London. Have you been there yourself recently?"

Her shot paid off as Anthony searched for words. "Ah. Unlike you, I never planned on rusticating here forever."

"Yes, I suppose not." Winter bit back her accusations. "Seen Lord Hollingsworth, mayhap?"

Derik's eyes narrowed, "Mayhap. Why?"

"Did he not tell you he propositioned me?"

Her childhood bane made an effort to appear unconcerned. "All is fair where a lady bird is concerned. Why should I care when you refuse my perfectly good offer."

Winter's eyes flashed. "Lady bird? Then you know he did not offer marriage."

Lord Derik stared at her. "It does not signify. Time you and I come to an understanding. Once we do, you need not concern yourself about the sort of options men like Hollingsworth offer. I can protect you from such as him."

"What are you going to do, drag me kicking and screaming to the altar?"

His eyes glittering, Anthony grabbed her arm. "Stop toying with me, Winter. I know what I want, and I want you as my wife. If you recall anything from our childhood, you know, one way or another, I get what I want or else."

"Or else destroy it," she finished in a whisper. *Lord, help me.* She looked Lord Derik in the eye. "I will not marry you, Anthony. Not ever. Do you think I will ever forget how you treated me after the accident? I was devastated. It was because of you Father began to shelter me."

"I was but a child."

"A reprehensible child and an evil, cold-hearted man."

The viscount's face darkened with fury, he gripped her arm until he left a bruise. "You'll regret those words, Winter."

Alistair returned exhausted, but satisfied with the information he managed to acquire. He accomplished his mission, found time to check on the manager at the Renton estate and to spend time at his own country seat. With some discreet inquiries, he found he had some very interesting neighbors.

Still, the mission took longer than planned, and he wished he had given Winter some explanation for his actions. He wondered if she had gone to services with his aunt, but thought not. Winter had a right to be angry with him, he decided. She would probably demand to be taken directly home.

He could see her drawing to her full height, eyes flashing, chin jutting out, reading him the riot act. He doubted a simple, "Forgive me," would do. Strange, not long past he would not have even considered her feelings on the matter. When did Winter take such a hold on his heart?

The minister's declaration sounded. "You cannot center your life on anything but Jesus Christ. Everything else will fail you."

He smiled. However many times he failed Winter, he doubted she would ever fail him. Her innocent love held him captive and her faith was holding more and more appeal.

Almost he had the coachman drive him home, but knew there was one other thing he must take care of first: a visit to the secretary. Melton sat nearby behind a desk.

The secretary appeared haggard. "Lord Alistair. Though your *Arabella* slid through again, our other run met with disaster. We suspect sabotage. Our ship sprung a very large and suspicious leak and limped back to port before getting halfway across the channel."

He stared at Alistair. "I hear tales of British citizens starving, men, women and children hiding like fugitives to keep from being hauled away to unspeakable horrors in some French prison. It is untenable!" His fist crashed down on the table before him.

"We have brought out several families. Our runs will continue."

The secretary sighed. "I doubt history will even record the importance of this work or the bravery of those who have undertaken the task. Mayhap they will never know." He smiled ruefully. "What about Mary?"

"So far, the information we have fed her—slightly too late for use—has kept them happy." Alistair rifled a hand through already disheveled hair. "I did discover some interesting things. Seems Hollingsworth's fiancée is a colorless little French miss entirely under the domination of her father, the Count Abjour.

"The count has quite the tale of evading his own people to come to England, and he is 'ever so grateful' to our country for taking him in. Personally, I cannot imagine what that daughter of his had to offer a man like Hollingsworth, unless her father has some hold on him."

The secretary nodded toward Viscount Melton, who shuffled through the papers on the desk, handing one to the secretary. Somberly the secretary handed the sheet to Alistair. A low whistle escaped from Alistair's lips as he scanned it.

"So Hollingsworth was deep in dun territory until his prospective father-in-law bought up his vowels. This might be the key. Surely he didn't need do that just to provide his daughter with a bridegroom."

"It has been done before."

"But why Hollingsworth? The two will not suit. Besides I would think Viscount Derik would have been a nearer target. He, too, is in debt from what I have discovered, though not as deeply."

"Unless—" the secretary let out a sigh before continuing "—he was looking for something more."

"Blackmail?"

"Ugly word, that. Think Hollingsworth would betray his fellow Horse Guards?"

Sucking in a deep breath, Alistair let it out slowly. "The man is a rake and a bounder, but a traitor...I can't say."

"Won't be easy catching him out. Mayhap, he simply gets his friends who are in places of security into their cups and pumps them for information. They would have no reason to believe him anything but a fellow soldier."

"Any leads?" Alistair scanned the paper again.

"We have spoken to everyone directly involved, but have turned up no solid leads. Whoever is passing on our secrets isn't about to divulge it. Could be, after a night with Hollingsworth, most don't recall what was divulged."

"If Hollingsworth is being blackmailed, he in turn may be blackmailing one of your people."

"My thoughts exactly. What about Lady Renton?"

"I warned her away from him."

"Don't underestimate either Hollingsworth or Derik. Both could use her against you."

"Are you saying she could be in some danger?"

"It's possible." The secretary handed Alistair another sheet. "Here's a list of British citizens we believe still to be in France."

"That is quite a list." He pointed to several marked in red ink. "These the ones?"

"They're waiting for you."

Getting up, Alistair tucked the list into the pocket of his jacket. "The *Arabella* makes a run tonight, as planned. Pray there'll be no trouble."

After meeting with the captain of his ship and handing over the information, Alistair headed home. Lord Alistair leaped from the carriage before it came to a complete stop and hurried into the house. He stopped first in the library hoping to encounter Winter, but the large room was silent and dark. He felt a vague disquiet at the silence.

"The duchess," James intoned from behind him, "is out for the afternoon."

"Very good, James, thank you." Alistair dismissed the man. Of course Winter was with his aunt. For some time he worked at his desk, reading reports, making notes and catching up with his correspondence.

Whistling tunelessly, Alistair ran up the staircase to his room, where his valet waited for him. After a long hot bath, he dressed in his evening clothes and went downstairs. He found his aunt about to enter the dining parlour.

Pecking her on the cheek, he said, "I see you got back from your afternoon outing all right. Where is Winter? Shouldn't we wait for her?"

Something in her sharp gaze gave him pause. She told James they would be along in a moment. "Justin."

"What is it? Is Winter ill?"

"Your ward is no longer here."

His insides congealed with fear. "Not here? Where is she?"

"She went home, Justin." She raised her hand to stem his protest. "After you left, I knew she was unhappy, though she tried hard not to show it."

Alistair grimaced, but let his aunt continue. "The other afternoon she ran into Hollingsworth while out riding that horse of hers. She was in a dither when she returned and nothing could stop her. She didn't even tell me until she was packed and ready to leave."

"You could have…"

"Stopped her? I don't think so. But I did insist she take Mary and Terrance." The duchess sighed. "She was in a taking about something."

"I can imagine. Did Hollingsworth frighten her? Surely she did not ride unescorted."

"I had made it known that Terrance would always accompany her. You could speak with him."

Reaching the bell pull, Alistair gave it a jerk. When the

butler answered the summons, he told him, "I want to see Carlyle, now."

A few minutes later, Carlyle sauntered jauntily into the room and took a seat without leave of either the earl or the duchess. Alistair smiled indulgently at the younger man. "I understand you escorted my ward on her rides."

"I did. Good hands, good seat. That horse of hers is a handful, but he is a kitten in her hands. Bet the two could give you and your roan a good run." He grinned.

"Impertinent as always," said Alistair, but his dry tone was belied by a grin. "Truth to tell, she did give me a good run in the country." His smile faded. "But I want to know what happened to make her leave so precipitously. Did Hollingsworth do or say anything to frighten her?"

Carlyle studied the earl's dark face. "Like that is it," he murmured before answering. "What can I say?"

"I want to know everything that happened."

"All right." Carlyle settled more comfortably as Alistair leaned against the mantel. "He insinuated she was dallying with me, first of all. Accused me—" he grinned before adding "—of being from the wrong side of the blanket."

Alistair started. "He didn't suspect?"

"I don't think so, but Winter certainly looked at me rather queerly." He paused, continued. "Hollingsworth told her you were out chasing your 'bit o'muslin' as he put it. Told her you might besmirch her innocence, but never offer marriage any more than he would."

Alistair's face darkened and despite his attempt at control, his hands fisted. "Go on."

Carlyle cleared his throat. "He said you'd be subtle with a hug, a touch, you know. That sort of thing."

Alistair's face paled. *No wonder she headed for the safety of Renton Hall.*

When the younger man hesitated, Alistair growled, "Out with it."

"The blackguard asked if you'd already had her."

The duchess gasped, and Alistair paced the floor. "I'll kill him. How dare he!"

"She's a brave one, your Winter, Justin. She stopped the man from flogging both his animal and his poor groom. You might like to know the horse dumped him neatly onto the ground. Such language."

This did not placate the earl. "Aunt Helen, how long has she been gone?"

"A week…" She glanced toward Carlyle for confirmation. He nodded.

"Terrance, get the roan saddled. There is no time to lose. I must go to Winter."

The groom got to his feet. "Be ready within the hour, Justin."

"Make it sooner."

"I think you should see Mary before you go." The younger man nodded as he exited.

His aunt regarded him carefully. "Are you in love with the girl, Justin?"

Alistair swung away sharply to hide the expression on his face. "Later, Aunt Helen. I must go to Winter. She could be in danger. First I have to find Mary."

Jupiter cantered up the well-worn path to Renton Hill. Mutton-head raced alongside the horse.

In the past couple of days, Winter had found a measure of peace. Without the intrusion of shopping and receptions and balls and teas, she spent time in the Word and in seeking God's guidance.

Her prayers often turned to her guardian. "Will he be angry with me, Lord? Or will he be relieved I am gone?"

That thought pained her, for far away from his presence, she found her love for him growing rather than diminishing.

Winter sighed. Would she ever forget his eyes gazing into hers, his hug, his strong arms?

A sharp retort shattered her reverie as Jupiter, screaming in pain, reared. Unprepared, Winter grabbed for the mane, missed and tumbled from the saddle. Her head hit a small outcropping of rock and blood spurted from the jagged cut in her forehead.

Whining, Mutton-head licked her face, but she lay still.

Around midnight, Alistair stopped at a posting inn, but after a few hours of tossing in his bed he resumed his ride. Anxiety drove him onward. Something was amiss. Though he told himself his disquiet was solely in his mind, he knew differently.

The world he had created for himself spun out of control. If something happened to Winter, life would not be worth living. He sucked in a breath. Had his life begun to revolve around her? What if she wanted nothing more to do with him? His heart sank.

"Oh, God," he groaned. There was no one else to turn to. He sensed Winter was in danger, and he must get to her as soon as possible.

Midafternoon, the earl swung off the heaving roan and ran up to the colonnaded porch. Duncan opened the door.

"Winter. Where is Lady Renton?"

"She is riding," Duncan informed him. "Up the hill, I believe she said."

"Thank you, Duncan." Hurrying back to the tired roan, he swung aboard.

Patting the sweating animal, he said, "Sorry, but our errand isn't finished yet."

The animal snorted as though understanding and headed up Renton Hill. The earl prayed he wasn't making a fool out of himself. Once he reached the summit, he began to pray in earnest.

He heard the dog's frantic yipping, then a growl, a snap of the jaws. A curse followed. Slowing the roan, he walked the animal to the edge of the clearing. Head down, Jupiter stood trembling, his front legs apart, the reins trailing. Blood trickled from the animal's hindquarters. Jupiter was nuzzling Winter, who lay unmoving on the ground.

To the side, Viscount Derik cursed loudly as he made another attempt to get close to the girl. Derik used a large branch to swipe at the dog, who growled and circled, always keeping the viscount from his mistress.

A pistol lay under the horse, successfully keeping it out of the viscount's reach. "Go away!" He waved his arms.

Jupiter shied, but refused to leave Winter. Derik dived for the gun and rolled away. Getting up, he pointed it straight at the inert girl.

Surging forward, Alistair leaped from the roan and grabbed Derik. Wrestling the gun from his hand, Alistair tossed it over the crest of the hill. Pulling the surprised viscount around, Alistair smashed his fist into his face. Derik dropped and lay still.

Leaving him lay, Alistair knelt beside Winter. Turning her over slowly, he gasped at the blood pouring down her face. There was so much blood Alistair found it difficult to assess her condition. He needed something clean.

Ripping a strip from her petticoats, he wiped the blood from her face, then probed gently until he found the jagged wound on her forehead. Shrugging out of his jacket, he rolled it up and placed it under her head.

His lips tight, Alistair ripped another strip from her petticoat to hold firmly over the gash in her head until the flow of blood eased. Quickly ripping several more strips, he folded them awkwardly and improvised a bandage around her head.

Still, Winter had not moved. Unbuttoning her jacket, Alistair laid his hand lightly over her heart. "Thank You, Lord," he murmured, feeling the slow, rhythmic beat.

He patted Mutton-head, who whined, then licked his face. "We're taking her home," he told the animal. With a bark, the dog started down the trail, turned and waited for Alistair to follow.

Catching up Jupiter's reins, he tied them over the saddle. When he probed the wound on the horse's side, Jupiter danced away skittishly. A cursory examination convinced the earl the wound was only a flesh wound. He prayed Winter's wound would also not prove serious. "Please, Lord, let her be all right." Prayer already didn't seem so strange on his lips. Something had definitely changed inside.

With another long strip from Winter's petticoat, Alistair tied Derik's hands together and threw him over Jupiter's saddle. Turning to Winter, he tenderly lifted her onto the roan and held her while he mounted. Cradling her in his arms, he gathered the reins.

"Jupiter," he called, hoping the horse would follow him back to the stables.

Blood seeped through Winter's makeshift bandage. By the time they arrived, blood was making rivulets down her cheeks and soaked Alistair's shirt and breeches. Mutton-head sounded the alarm.

A young groom came running. At the sight of his mistress unconscious and bloody, the groom yelled for help. Gingerly, he took the woman from Alistair's arms and lowered her to the ground. Another took the roan.

"Someone get the doctor," commanded the earl, and he saw a groom run for a horse.

A stable boy carried the news to the hall, bringing the housekeeper. "My poor child. My little lamb."

Alistair soothed, "She's alive, Mrs. Duncan."

Another groom held Jupiter, who pranced and shied until Alistair pulled the viscount from his back. Derik swayed dizzily, groggily trying to focus his eyes.

Shaking him, Alistair shouted, "What were you doing on Renton Hill?"

Sullenly Derik answered. "Trying to help, that's all."

The earl's gaze penetrated his false bravado. "I saw you point the gun at her."

"No, I was merely going to wing that fool dog so I could get close enough to help her."

"Will Winter tell the same story when she wakes up?"

Fear flitted across Derik's features. "If she wakes up."

Alistair clenched his fist. How he wanted to pound the insolent peer into the ground, but he glanced toward Winter and pushed the viscount away. Derik was right. He had no real proof.

"Don't you ever, I repeat, ever put one foot on Renton land again." He turned to a nearby groom. "Give him a horse and let him go."

"What about my horse?" Derik straightened his jacket.

Alistair glared. "We'll send it along later." Though the viscount made a show of indifference as he mounted the less-than-prime animal brought for him, Alistair noticed that his hands shook.

Kneeling, he lifted Winter and carried his light burden into the house, where he followed Mrs. Duncan to Winter's bedchamber. She closed the door behind them after giving orders to the flustered housemaids.

Alistair said, "We have to get her out of this habit."

"We? It is not seemly for you."

"This is no time for false modesty. We're talking about her life. Now are you going to help me or must I do this myself?"

"At least turn your back."

By the time he turned around, Winter was under the covers and had begun to shiver. He watched as the housekeeper deftly cleaned her wound. The cut still oozed and, while the housekeeper folded a bandage for Winter's head, Alistair held a clean cloth against it. Winter stirred, but did not awaken.

Before the housekeeper was ready with the bandage, the old family doctor briskly strode into the room. Moving aside, the earl let the doctor take his place beside Winter.

Dr. Morgan, a man of quiet efficiency, examined the wound. "Any other injuries?" he asked on being told of the situation.

"There don't appear to be," Alistair responded. Noting the doctor's raised eyebrow, he declared, "I am the girl's guardian."

"Never thought she needed one," the doctor grunted, expertly bandaging Winter's head.

"I don't want her left alone," he said, turning around. "She has a concussion."

Mrs. Duncan gulped. "Will she come out of it?"

"Hard to tell." The doctor sighed. "We know so little about head wounds."

Alistair frowned. "What can we do?"

"Stay with her…and pray." Wiping his hands, he repacked his bag. "If she comes around, send for me. Otherwise, I'll be back first thing tomorrow."

The housekeeper moved toward the bed. "I'll sit with her."

"No, I'll stay." Alistair firmly pulled up a hard chair and sat down. "I am staying."

"I'll spell you later," said the housekeeper, but Alistair scarcely heard.

Tenderly he touched Winter's cheek. "Winter, you have to wake up. Tiger, fight. You have to fight." Closing his eyes, he began to pray.

Chapter 12

The afternoon slipped behind the horizon, and still Winter did not stir. Alternately, Alistair prayed and talked to Winter.

"'Tiger, Tiger, burning bright,'" he quoted slowly, "'in the forests of the night...'"

He continued quoting, his own eyes misting as he continued.

"'When the stars threw down their spears, and watered heaven with their tears, did He smile His work to see? Did He who made the Lamb make thee?'"

"'Tiger, Tiger, burning bright...'"

Swallowing with some difficulty, he finished the poem almost as a prayer.

"Winter, fight. You must fight. Lord, You made the lamb, and You made Winter. I know You love her, and now that You have put this love in my heart for her, please don't take her away." He had his head cradled in his arms, praying, when the housekeeper tiptoed into the room.

She lightly touched his shoulder and spoke with compassion. "M'lord?"

Alistair jerked up, blinked. "Mrs. Duncan."

"You're exhausted, Lord Alistair. Dinner is ready. I'll stay with Lady Renton."

When Alistair protested, she put her hands on her wide hips. "You'll do my mistress no good falling asleep. You need to eat, and," she said, eyeing his rumpled bloodstained clothes, "you need to freshen up."

A grin quirked the corners of his mouth at her imperious tone. "I'll eat, and then return."

"Not until you change clothes, you won't. Why, if my lady woke up, the sight of you would make her swoon. Not that she ever did before, mind you."

For the first time, Alistair regarded his clothes. Sniffed. "Dreadful. Oh, yes. Quite dreadful."

"Don't worry. They brought in your things, and you can bathe and change before you eat."

"Thanks." He found a bath waiting and, with relief, cleaned up and put on the freshly pressed breeches, shirt and jacket laid out on the bed. He found his travel bag, which had been attached to the back of his saddle, tucked in the corner.

Feeling more the thing, Alistair joined Mr. Jonas in the dining parlour. As they ate, Mr. Jonas asked hesitantly, "How is Lady Renton?"

"Concussion," Alistair told him.

Again the manager hesitated, until Alistair grew irritated. "Out with it, man."

"I've been making some discreet inquiries, m'lord."

The earl looked up, "About?"

"Lord Derik."

Alistair waited for Mr. Jonas to continue, giving no clue to what he either knew or suspected.

"Seems his lordship's estate is in financial difficulties. Gambling. He needs the blunt to pull it out."

Fingering the stem of his glass, Alistair answered, "I am convinced he caused her accident."

"If I may be so bold—what was he trying to do?"

"I have two theories. Either he hoped she would be injured, and he could be her knight in shining armor, or…"

"Or," Mr. Jonas prompted.

Alistair's face darkened. "He meant to murder her. He may think she knows something he doesn't want passed on."

"What's he going to do now?"

"Don't worry. I am going to see to it he no longer has reason to pursue her with marriage in mind."

Alistair found the housekeeper comfortably ensconced on a deep-cushioned chair.

"I am clean and fed," said Alistair. "Do I pass as a sitter for a time?"

A stubborn light shown in the woman's eyes. "I daresay you haven't slept much the past few nights. You need sleep."

As though in answer, Alistair stifled a yawn. "Bother! Mayhap a few hours. How is she?"

"The same. She hasn't moved." A sob escaped the large woman's lips.

Feeling awkward, Alistair patted her shoulder. "We'll keep praying, Mrs. Duncan. He does hear us. Oh, yes. I'll relieve you in a few hours."

He felt her gaze on his back as he left the room and heard her quiet "Well, praise be!"

In his spacious room, Alistair blew out the candles and settled with a sigh into the comfortable bed. It wasn't long before his eyes closed. Deep in the stillness of the night he awoke, groggy with sleep. He heard the grandfather clock in the hallway bong, once, twice, three times.

Alistair forced himself to get up. A few minutes later he made his way down the hall.

Mrs. Duncan's hands, wrapped in her crochet work, lay forgotten on her lap. Her head bobbed against the back of the chair with each loud snore.

Alistair tapped the woman's shoulder. "Mrs. Duncan, wake up."

Jerking awake, the housekeeper stared at Alistair. "Oh, dear, don't tell me I fell asleep. Her ladyship?"

Alistair bent over Winter, felt the pulse in her neck. "No change." He turned. "You go on to bed."

As the door closed behind her, Alistair took her place in the chair. Leaning over, he stroked Winter's soft cheek. "Wake up, tiger," he coaxed. "Wake up."

Sometime later, he shot forward at her murmur. "Bit o'muslin. Bit o'muslin. Justin." She groaned. "Love. No."

"Winter." He kept his voice soft. "Winter?"

Suddenly her eyes flew open. Her eyes widened at seeing Justin leaning over her, his face anxious. "Justin, you're here." Before he could respond, her eyes closed.

Taking her hand, Alistair held it to his lips. "I am here, my tiger. I won't leave you again. Do you hear me, Winter? I am here." She did not respond.

When Dr. Morgan stopped in the next morning, Alistair told him, "She opened her eyes and muttered a few words during the night. She recognized me. The next moment she was out again."

"Good. Looks like she may be coming out of it. Don't leave her alone." After changing the bandage, the doctor left.

Winter wavered in and out of consciousness for the next two days. Times of lucidity never lasted more than a moment or two, but Winter seemed to be gaining in strength.

Alistair and Mrs. Duncan regularly spelled one another. During the long hours of inactivity, Alistair picked up Winter's bible and spent long hours absorbing its message. He put it down with reluctance as though parting from a beloved friend.

Each time the housekeeper relieved him, Alistair found it more and more difficult to leave.

"I can stay longer."

"Now, m'lord," the housekeeper declared, "I know you care about her, but it will do her no good if you wear yourself out. You need a break, and there are a couple of prime cattle that need exercise."

"You're right, Mrs. Duncan. I do believe you're worse than my nanny—the bane of my young life." He softened his words with a grin.

"Have done with your flummery," Mrs. Duncan said. "Now off with you. If she awakes, I'll let you know."

Late the third morning, Winter opened her eyes, her mind clear. "Justin."

Alistair, who had been up most of the night, snapped awake. "Winter?"

"I didn't dream you." Weakly she reached a hand to touch his cheek as he leaned over toward her.

Alistair's heart began to pound. A boyish grin spread across his face. "You're back!"

She smiled.

He jerked the bell cord. Mrs. Duncan hurried into the room. "Winter, is she…?"

"She's awake," Alistair cried. "She's going to make it!"

"Praise be!" Mrs. Duncan pulled out a kerchief and dabbed at her eyes. Straightening, she said, "You need nourishment, m'lady. I'll see to it immediately."

Going to the windows, Alistair pulled back the curtains to let in the morning light before sitting down on the edge of the bed. Taking Winter's hand, he kissed it. The two gazed at each other, exchanging things too deep for mere words.

When the housekeeper returned, Alistair reluctantly stepped aside to give her room at Winter's bedside. As he watched Mrs.

Duncan feed Winter spoonful by spoonful, he could almost see Winter's eyes brighten.

"Enough," she finally whispered and, with a soft smile, slipped into a deep, natural sleep.

Hours later, Winter awoke to find Alistair studying her. This time Winter frowned. "I thought you were busy. Lord Hollingsworth implied…"

"I am well aware of his Banbury tales. Did you truly credit his lies?" She saw disappointment in his eyes.

"You left me."

Alistair rifled his hand through his hair. "I haven't taken a woman to my bed since…since Amelia." Winter heard a hint of bitterness. "I thought you had begun to trust me, Winter."

"In the sitting room, you held me, said you cared…and left…."

"I should not have attended you at night, not even in your sitting room, Winter. I only thought about explaining the truth of the matter." He traced her cheek with his fingers, causing color to flame Winter's cheeks. "However, walking away was one of the most difficult things I have ever done."

"Justin…" Whatever she meant to say was forgotten as the door opened to admit Mrs. Duncan carrying a tray.

"M'lady, more soup."

Winter struggled to sit up. Reaching down, Alistair put his arms around her and pulled her up. Winter shivered at his touch.

Putting down the tray, the housekeeper shooed Alistair from the room. "Luncheon is waiting to be served for you, as well."

Bowing in mock surrender, Alistair shook his head in mock dismay. "Upon my word, the woman has been ordering me around ever since I arrived."

"Stuff and nonsense," the housekeeper said, "someone has to keep you in line. Always hoverin' over her ladyship like some lovesick calf."

Winter caught the twitch in Alistair's cheek. Could it possibly be? But after a short laugh, he exited without comment.

When Mrs. Duncan put the spoon into the thick soup, Winter took it from her. "Here, I can do that."

Under the housekeeper's watchful eye, Winter managed to empty the bowl. "Delicious." She put down the spoon and leaned back. "When did Lord Alistair get here?"

"Why, miss. His lordship found you on Renton Hill days ago. All bloody you was. No dandy, that one. Didn't mind his fine coat in his concern for you. He brought you down all cradled in his arms. I've had to force him to leave your side to take care of himself. He was in a case, he was."

Winter's eyes widened. "Truly?"

"You know I don't tell tales."

"I know, Mrs. Duncan. Sorry." A silly grin came to her lips. He really did care!

A few minutes later, Winter slid down into the covers and was once more asleep.

Alistair was by Winter's side when she awoke later that afternoon. "You're awake. How do you feel?"

"Passable. Nasty headache."

"The doctor said you'll be fine now if you take it easy for a few days yet."

"He was here then?"

"Less than an hour ago." Alistair touched her cheek. "I need to talk with you, Winter. Are you up to a few questions?"

She nodded, but seemed to find it difficult to concentrate when he touched her.

"What happened on the hill? What did you see, hear?"

Closing her eyes, Winter spoke slowly. "Hoofbeats. I heard hoofbeats. Then a shot of some kind. Something hit Jupiter. I wasn't ready when he reacted."

"Why would someone want to hurt you?"

He witnessed realization in her eyes. "What is it? What do you know? You must tell me, Winter."

"I...I don't want to accuse anyone. I didn't see anyone."

"But you think you know who, don't you? Was it Derik?"

Winter began to tremble, and Alistair slipped a reassuring arm about her shoulders. "Tell me about Derik."

"Yes, I think it was Anthony. I...I did hear something, but not then. When I first returned home. I didn't know what to do. I didn't know how to reach you."

"I know and I am sorry about that, but I am here now."

Tensing, Winter pulled away and searched his face. "How do you feel about Mary? I've seen you together."

"Hmm." He eyed her, wondering how much to tell her.

"Are you in love with her?"

"Certainly not."

"She is a spy, Justin. I heard her with Derik."

This time Alistair stiffened. "How do you know this?"

"Mary and her husband accompanied me home. That night I overheard her and Anthony in the garden talking."

Alistair's voice hardened. "Did Anthony know you heard him?"

"It's possible." She sucked in a deep breath as though to steady herself. "I found out why he wanted to m-marry me."

"I know."

She stared into his face. "You know...how?"

"Mary told me."

"But she's a spy!"

"Yes, but for us, dearest, for us."

Winter slumped against the pillows. "I am so glad. She isn't just a maid, is she?"

"No, darling Winter." He sighed, touched her cheek, his gaze soft again. "Mary is my sister-in-law."

"Then Carlyle is..."

"My brother. Yes. Hollingsworth was closer to the truth than he knew. Actually he did spend some years in India, where he started to do undercover work for the government. When he was asked to do the same at home, we put out the rumor that he had died overseas."

"Mary is a spy, too?"

"Hiding out for the time being." He paused, then decided nothing but the full truth would do. "We have been trying to discover who is involved in stealing secrets and handing them over to the French. There is a leak somewhere."

Winter gasped. "Our own people betraying us?"

"I fear so."

"Lord Derik is one of them, isn't he?" He could tell from her expression something suddenly clicked. "Do you think Hollingsworth is part of this?"

"Why do you ask?"

"The things he said to me. I suppose you keep private information in the library. That's why he wanted to go there. I knew there had to be a reason." She lowered her face.

Alistair lifted her quivering chin. "You have a very special loveliness, Winter. Two more questions, if I may."

Feeling her weakness overcoming her, Winter nodded.

Slowly, his eyes on her face, he asked, "Do you still care for me? And, will you return to London with me?"

"I was wrong to leave as I did, Justin, and I am sorry," Winter whispered. "I'll do as you ask. I thought it would be the same when I came back, but nothing has been the same. I don't belong here any longer. I don't belong anywhere. I do not understand God's plan at all."

Her pain twisted his insides. "Oh, Winter. You do belong. God loves you very much." He smiled. "You may not think so, but your faith and the words of the minister did bear fruit. I had a lot of time to get things straightened out with the Lord on the journey here. You see, you have been a witness for Him."

Tears gathered in her eyes. "Justin, you came back to Jesus."

"I did."

"Oh, Justin!" she cried as he gathered her in his arms.

Releasing her, he laid her gently against the pillows. "Are you tired, darling?"

"Happy." Yawning, she admitted sheepishly, "Well, a little tired."

Kissing her cheek, Alistair ordered, "Go to sleep, my little tiger. When you awake mayhap you'll feel more the thing."

"Are you going away again?"

"Not for long, darling, not for long."

"I love you, Justin," she murmured, her eyes closing. "Welcome to God's family."

That afternoon, the housekeeper and another maid helped her bathe. While Mrs. Duncan helped her into a fresh nightgown, a maid changed the bed.

Again she slept, not knowing Alistair had taken the roan and headed toward his country estate.

Chapter 13

Lord Alistair detoured to see Lord Derik. "How is she?" the viscount asked, pouring himself a drink from the grog tray in the corner. The viscount sat down, careful not to wrinkle his pantaloons.

Alistair sat unbidden opposite in a cane-back chair. "She will recover."

Tossing down his drink, Derik faced Alistair. "I see. Does that precipitate the pleasure of this visit?"

"If you must know, it is more than that. I believe you well know Lady Renton overheard you and Mary talking in the garden. When Winter refused to marry you, the only other option was to silence her—permanently."

Lord Derik smiled faintly. "You'll never prove that."

"Does it matter? All I need do is bring to the attention of the secretary your verbal admission of collusion with the French, and you will hang as a traitor."

Lord Derik's face paled, and his hand crept up to his neck.

"Knowing that, you came to confront me. What if you disappeared?"

"You think I am so addle-brained as to come without letting my people know what I am about? As for Mary, how much would she take before she cracked?"

Wiping beads of sweat from his brow, Derik growled, "What do you want?"

"I want the truth. Who is behind this operation?"

Derik looked away. He paused as if considering, then said, "Count Abjour approached me. He knew about my gambling, my debts and a few other indiscretions. He didn't threaten outright. Instead, he talked about how I could see the return of my mother's estates, if I did something now and again for him."

"He outright said that Boney would restore land to you if you could prove you were of the French aristocracy?"

"That's the right of it. All I had to do was to pass on some papers, which came my way now and again."

"Anything else?"

Derik pursed his lips. "I did have to provide for a gentleman or two whom I suspected were French spies. I gave them food and clothing and got them to London."

"The papers, did you read any of them?"

"No." He frowned. "Whatever you think of me, I really didn't want to betray this country, but once I was in…"

"The count kept sucking you in further. Who else is involved?"

Licking his lips, Derik glanced at the high ceiling then back. "I had no other contacts."

Alistair sensed he lied. "If you think anyone will help you, forget it. We're onto the operation now, and we're bringing you all down."

Standing up, Alistair towered over the other man. "My suggestion is that you, personally, take over your French estates, before this one is taken from you."

He stepped toward the door, turned. "I wouldn't contact the count, if I were you, or you might not get a chance to leave the country."

Winter awoke to find the housekeeper sitting with her. "Where's Lord Alistair?"

"He is gone." At the dejected look on Winter's face, Mrs. Duncan hastened to add, "He had some pressing business to attend, but plans on returning first thing in the morning."

She wondered if his business had ought to do with the information she had imparted to him.

That evening she got up, and, with the housekeeper's assistance, washed her hair, bathed and sat up for a couple of hours before retiring for the night.

Despite the woman's protestations, Winter refused to be watched over during the night. Almost as soon as Mrs. Duncan closed the door of the darkened room, Winter, breathing a prayer for Justin's safety, fell asleep.

He had not yet returned when she awoke the next morning, and it was hard not to show the disappointment she felt. Had what he said about not leaving her, about committing his life to Christ, been true? She recalled, too, the endearments. What did they mean?

The doctor's visit cheered her somewhat. "With rest, you are going to be fine, young lady."

After a short rest, Winter walked around the room and stared out the open window at the riot of flowers and trees. Closing her eyes, she breathed in the fragrance of carefully tended roses and a variety of other flowers she could not identify.

When Mrs. Duncan brought a substantial luncheon on a tray, she found she did full justice to the meal.

"Has Lord Alistair returned?"

"He has," said Mrs. Duncan, taking the tray and setting it

outside the door. She marched to the armoire. "Let's see. What shall you wear?"

"Anything will do," Winter told her, trying unsuccessfully to quell a grin. Yawning, she added, "Mayhap I should rest a while and dress later. I'd like to go to the dining hall for dinner."

Winter awoke feeling better than she had in days. She found Mrs. Duncan laying out an evening gown. "I do not need to look all that fancy."

The housekeeper's eyes twinkled. "Not even for your guardian?"

Blushing, Winter slid out of bed, freshened up and let the housekeeper assist her into the cool silk gown with sleeves that puffed from shoulder to elbow. A wide black sash encircled her high-waisted gown.

Mrs. Duncan unwrapped the bandage from around Winter's head and brushed out the long silvery hair before putting on a fresh, thinner bandage.

"You are an angel, m'lady," the housekeeper told her, seeming awed by the transformation.

"Hardly," Winter said, but was nonetheless pleased with the results.

"I agree, she is an angel," said Alistair, from the doorway.

Swinging to face him, Winter turned too quickly and felt herself falling. Alistair's arms closed about her. "Dearest." Winter felt the quick staccato of his heart.

Dizzy, Winter closed her eyes until the spell passed. She opened them to find him peering down at her anxiously. "Are you all right?"

Her smile wobbled. "I felt dizzy momentarily, but I am fine now."

"Mayhap I should carry you." His concern sent a shiver of warmth down her spine.

"I'd like to walk, if I may."

While Mrs. Duncan hurried from the room muttering some

excuse Winter did not catch, Alistair tucked her arm in his. Dressed in formal evening wear of black superfine jacket and breeches, Alistair fair took Winter's breath away.

With Alistair gazing down into her face, Winter took no notice of their direction until they entered the sitting room next to her bedroom. Supper was laid out with candles and flowers.

Lord Alistair carefully pulled out an ornate cushioned chair and seated her beside the table for two, before seating himself.

Winter glanced around. "Why here and not the dining room?"

Lord Alistair squeezed her hand. "For one, Mrs. Duncan feared you were not up to the walk to and from the dining room. She would not allow me to carry you." His grin was impish.

"Oh. This is rather nice." She glanced around as Mr. and Mrs. Duncan served them. "Seems rather formal nonetheless."

Lord Alistair exchanged a glance with the housekeeper that made Winter wonder. "Just you eat, m'lady."

Awake, feeling better than she had in days and with the marked attentions of her handsome guardian, Winter chose to do just that. However, when Mrs. Duncan removed the last of the dishes after the main course and Mr. Duncan blew out most of the candles before they left, Winter became more than a little suspicious.

"Justin," Winter asked, "what's this all about?"

Lord Alistair took her hand and led her to the settee in front of the hearth. Taking her hands in his, he searched her face. "I asked the Duncans to decorate, serve and make tonight special."

"I…I don't understand." Winter stuttered the words while her heart began to beat a little faster. Was it possible?

Justin's expression held such tenderness as he told her, "I wanted tonight to be memorable." He paused. "I love you, Winter, and I think you love me. I am asking you to be my wife."

Winter swallowed and swallowed again. "Y-you want to marry me?"

"Very much. If you will have me. I know I only recently returned to my faith, but…"

Winter bit her lip. She had to know. "What about Lady Bridget? She is so beautiful," Winter whispered.

Justin drew her close. "Oh, my darling Winter. You refine too much on her attentions. She may dress in the mode and have high-flown airs, but there is little of substance beneath the first stare of fashion."

"She wants you for herself.…"

Alistair ran a gentle finger down her pale cheek. "But I do not want her. I have been polite, nothing more. Please believe me when I say, once you came into my life there has been no room for anyone else—regardless of their wiles. I love you, Winter." Concern crossed his face. "You do believe me?"

Winter searched his face and her heart began to sing. He loved her! Letting out a long breath, she nodded. "I do, Justin."

His gentle smile drew her. "Now, how about an answer to my question. Will you marry me?"

"I love you, Justin." A radiance illuminated her face. "Yes. Yes, I will."

A grin plastered his face. "Then tonight we celebrate our engagement. Aunt Helen will be over the moon planning the wedding."

With aching tenderness, Alistair pulled Winter into his arms and kissed her soft lips.

The next moment, he released her and all but ran to the door. Flinging it open, he cried, "She said, 'Yes!'"

A few moments later, the Duncans brought in and served a beautifully decorated cake.

"When did Cook have the time?"

"They all love you, Winter, and when I told them what I had planned, everyone helped out."

Later, as they conversed, she told him about Derik. "It wasn't an accident."

"No, but Lord Derik won't hurt you again. Even now he is on his way to France."

Chapter 14

Two days later, Alistair assisted Winter into the Renton carriage, a long unused lumbering coach. She patted the worn squabs. "I remember when this carriage was in the first stare."

Alistair wrapped an arm around her shoulders. "As long as it gets us where we're going, does it matter?"

Shaking her head, Winter leaned against him. She still had headaches at times and her strength was not as it ought to be, but she was determined not to let Alistair know how tired she was from the preparation for the trip back to London.

As though sensing her concern, Alistair said, "I know I shouldn't have rushed you, but the season is almost over, and we have a wedding to plan."

He touched her head, still covered with a light bandage. "I did promise Dr. Morgan to take particular care of you."

Looking up into his face, Winter said, "I can't believe you can really want me as I am. I fear that one of these days I will awake to find this is nothing but a dream."

"Then let's make it a pleasant one, darling."

The day was long for Winter, who tired easily. By the time the carriage lumbered to a stop in front of Alistair House the next day, Winter was groggy from lack of sleep and aching in every muscle.

When Alistair lifted her from the coach, she released a sigh of relief. Holding her close, Alistair shifted her weight before carrying her up the wide front stairs into the house.

"Good to have you back, Lord Alistair. I hear congratulations are in order."

Winter glanced at Alistair. "I did not know you had sent word on ahead."

"With the season more than half over, it was imperative Aunt Helen know."

The duchess, descending the staircase at that moment, answered, "So little time to plan the wedding before everyone leaves for the summer." She hugged Winter. Noticing the bandage, she glanced toward her nephew. "What happened?"

"An accident, Aunt Helen. Winter is recovering nicely, but we must take care not to overtire her."

Though Winter tried to concentrate, her head buzzed, and she slumped weakly against Alistair. Picking her up, he said, "We'll talk later, Aunt Helen."

Upstairs, Alistair lay Winter down.

A scratch at the door drew him away, and he admitted Mary. "Mary, come in."

"Congratulations." She curtsied formally.

"She knows, Mary."

"She does?" With that, Mary gave Alistair a hug. "Congratulations from both of us."

Alistair led her to Winter. "Winter, may I present your future sister-in-law, Mary Stuart."

"Sorry I deceived you."

"I am glad to know the truth of the matter. I thought…"

"You were a French spy," said Alistair. "She overheard you talking with your cousin."

This time it was Mary who said, "Oh, my! Poor Anthony."

"Poor Anthony tried to murder my fiancée." He paused, then continued, "Since he was a close connection of yours, Mary, I gave him fair warning. He is now probably safely in France for the duration of the war."

"What about Terrance and me?"

"Mary, we still need your contacts and Terrance's undercover work until we put Count Abjour out of commission." He sighed. "I discovered the count is the one who turned in your parents. If he finds out who you are..."

Mary shrugged. "Well, at least I'll have time to get better acquainted with my future sister-in-law."

"As long as both of you remember that outside this room you are an abigail only." He touched Winter's cheek. "Winter is exhausted. I'll leave her to your ministrations, Mary. Winter—" his smile as well as his tender words overwhelmed her heart "—I'll have dinner sent up."

Later, over her protests, he called in a doctor to check her head. She winced as the doctor's long thin fingers probed her wound. Grunting his satisfaction, the doctor replaced the bandage with a patch. "You are healing nicely."

Gingerly, Winter felt her forehead. "Then I'll be all right?"

"You will always have a scar, but your hair should hide that, I believe." The tall, gaunt man straightened. "Lord Alistair, Lady Renton will need to take it easy for a while yet."

"I am taking good care of her, Doctor." True to his word, Alistair had Winter rest that afternoon. "I must be gone for a short while, but I'll return in time for dinner tonight." He gave her a kiss. "Now behave yourself, dearest."

From the window in her room, Winter watched Alistair take up the reins of a phaeton.

Hearing the door, she swung around to face the duchess. "Your grace."

"My dear, I think it is time you call me Aunt Helen, like the rest of the family."

Winter was overwhelmed. "You don't mind then that Justin asked me to marry him?"

The duchess tapped the gold-headed cane she used for effect on the floor. "About time, I'd say."

"I thought."

"Fustian! Don't you think I saw the way that nephew of mine looked at you?" She nodded. "You need to be fitted for your gown." By the time the duchess left, Winter felt rather dazed over all the woman's plans.

Alistair drove to White's, where he settled into an alcove with the secretary. The man ordered drinks for them both, then toasted Alistair. "I hear congratulations are in order."

Alistair leaned back and smiled laconically. "I suppose Mary also told you about Derik and his attempt on Lady Renton's life."

"She did. Looks like the situation is coming to a head, and none too soon. I fear the information being leaked now has to do with the strength and the size of our military build up. Carlyle is on the tail of the count. He is now in London."

Alistair started. "Here? I didn't figure he would dare show his hand in London."

The secretary shook his head. "Nor did I. But when you so precipitously deprived him of Derik, you evidently deprived him of his link with Hollingsworth. That's the way I see it."

"Then he isn't sure of Hollingsworth? Has my brother discovered anything to connect the count with the leaks? Something that will turn the tide?"

"Not yet, but," the secretary's eyes held amusement as he continued, "I fear you'll be deprived of a groom for the time being."

Alistair chuckled. "I've been told relations are notoriously unreliable as hired help anyway."

The secretary sobered. "So far, the count hasn't made contact with anyone we're watching, and we're keeping an especially close eye on Hollingsworth. Melton has become his particular friend. He's good, that one. We're also keeping an eye on Mary, for her protection, of course."

"I don't want her harmed." Alistair rifled his hair. "I am also concerned about my fiancée. I don't want her put in jeopardy. She has suffered enough."

"Then pray the count doesn't learn of her inadvertent involvement. For her sake, keep Hollingsworth away from her."

"I plan on staying close." A laconic smile touched his lips.

The secretary grinned. "Am I right to assume that will be no hardship?"

Alistair managed to keep a straight face. "I don't mind the sacrifice for my country, of course."

With that, Alistair took his leave. After making another important stop, Alistair directed his prime cattle to Alistair House. He found Mary readying Winter for the evening's affair.

Alistair surveyed Winter's figure-flattering sapphire-blue gown. The nearly off-the-shoulder neckline ended in short puff sleeves. His eyes glinted appreciatively.

"I like what you did with your bandage." He indicated the wide blue headband covering the patch over her wound.

"It was Mary's idea."

He smiled and addressed Mary. "Hopefully, before long, you and Terrance will take your proper place within society. First, we must make certain it is safe for you to do so."

Patting Winter's long skirt into place one last time, Mary said, "I'm more worried about Terrance than myself. I will be glad to have done with this charade." With a catch in her voice she hugged Winter.

"Oh, Justin. I wish she was going with us."

"I, too. Pray this will be over soon, but I don't want you

sad tonight." He pulled a small ornate box from his jacket and opened it.

Winter gasped. Sparkling against the dark velvet interior was a band inset with a large sapphire surrounded by tiny diamonds in the shape of a heart. "It is beautiful!"

Taking her trembling hand, Alistair slipped the ring on her finger. "I wanted you to have a special betrothal ring."

"Thank you, Justin. If this is a dream, I hope I never wake up." She held her hand so the ring sparkled in the candlelight. "I'll never take it off."

Leaning down, Alistair's mouth possessed hers until she clung to him. "I love you, my little tiger. Give me a few minutes and I'll be ready to escort my two ladies to the ball."

The duchess gracefully entered the silk-paneled saloon dressed in a dove-gray silk gown on the arm of Lord Alistair, debonair in a dark blue velvet jacket, gray waist and black breeches. On his other side walked Winter, head high, tense with anticipation.

Once inside, the duchess moved off to greet friends. Ignoring Winter, Lady Bridget moved quickly to Alistair's side. Glancing toward Winter, Alistair raised an eyebrow, a smile of annoyance on his lips.

Bridget simpered, "I missed you so."

"I had an important affair to attend to in the country."

The woman pouted. "Here the season is in full swing, and you've missed too much of it."

"Couldn't be helped." He disentangled himself from her grasp.

"Lady Bridget, I would like to present…"

"I have already been presented to your little ward."

"Hmm. But I do not think you have been presented to my fiancée." He winked at Winter.

Bridget's eyes glittered with cold fury. Collecting herself, she swallowed with some difficulty before cooing, "Congratulations, my dear Justin."

He frowned at her condescension. "I believe the duchess is finalizing plans for an announcement reception as well as the wedding."

"I am sure I'll have invitations then." Bridget's laughter had a decidedly hollow ring. "I'll have to check when I get home. I get so many," she said to Winter. "You know how it is."

Winter murmured some response and was relieved when Bridget excused herself. They watched her stop and heard the murmur rippling through the guests.

"Our wedding is now the latest on-dit, my dear," Alistair whispered. "I hope you're ready."

Soon the couple was surrounded by elegantly appointed lords and their ladies. Winter saw questions in the eyes of some and a stinging dart or two thrown out about the unexpected betrothal.

Lord Heywood raised his glass in a toast. "Not as big a shock as you might think, Alistair."

Winter smiled until her lips stuck to her teeth. As glass after glass was drunk to their health, Winter shifted uncomfortably. Alistair sensed her discomfort. "I do believe the congratulations are getting a mite too hearty and our well-wishers a bit too in their cups," he murmured for her ears alone.

A familiar figure found his way to Winter's side.

"Hollingsworth!" Alistair exclaimed, frowning.

"Don't get in a spin, Alistair." He bowed to Winter. "So congratulations are in order. I am devastated at the news."

His glare held malice. "Looks like you won this round, but don't count me out." He glanced toward her head as though he knew the band hid her wound. "A dream can end abruptly in the light of reality."

Winter shivered. Alistair didn't like the doubt that flickered in her eyes at the insinuation.

Alistair put his arm around her waist. "Leave her alone, Hollingsworth."

In his bow, Hollingsworth whispered, "Remember what I said, Winter."

The next morning, the duchess took Winter to the modiste for a final fitting on a gown she had ordered when she received word of the marriage.

"I went ahead without you, dear, since time matters," she explained as the coachman drove them to Bond Street in the open landau.

"I understand, and it is perfectly fine." Her voice was suddenly drowned out by a large pack of vicious mongrels darting into the street. Yipping and barking they nipped at the horses' heels.

The coachman, muttering an oath, snapped his whip at one of the dogs. With a yip, it darted under the vehicle, scaring the horses. Neighing, the horses reared in their traces, threatening not only to bolt, but also to tangle themselves in the silver-studded harness.

A man in a worn topcoat darted into the rutted roadway. Bearing a branch, he waded into the pack and managed to break up the attack. Reaching for the horses' bridles, he pulled them down. Murmuring to them, he calmed them enough for the coachman to regain control. The coachman nodded his thanks.

"My man," called the duchess, motioning the man forward. She dropped a few coins into his hand. "Thank you for your able assistance."

The man touched his battered hat. "'Twas nothin', ma'am. Glad to do it for the lady." He glanced toward Winter, his eyes widening.

Suddenly she recognized him. "You're Lord Hollingsworth's groom."

"Was, m'lady."

"He let you go?" Winter's eyes flashed. "Why?"

"After you intervened, m'lady. He turned myself and my family into the streets."

Furious, Winter explained the situation to the duchess. "Surely there is something we can do."

The duchess asked, "What is your name?"

"Abraham Danly, your grace."

Winter leaned toward him. "Where are you living now? Have you found work?"

"Been doin' odd jobs, but my lord spread around I stole from him, and no one wants to take me on, permanent-like."

The duchess asked, "Have you no place to live?"

Though reluctant to reveal the depth of his poverty, Winter and the duchess got him to answer their questions. Winter especially was horrified that the man, his wife and five children subsisted in the filthy backstreets of London. When she and the duchess returned to Alistair House, Winter sought out Alistair.

She found him bent over his desk. Quickly she summed up the situation for him. "Isn't there something we can do for him? Getting rid of those awful dogs may have saved our lives."

Alistair held her close. "I'm going to be afraid to let you out of my sight, dearest," He paused. "Other women beg for jewels and fripperies. You think only of others. Listen," he said and kissed her briefly, "the renters of the castle house recently lost the man who runs their stable, such as it is. How about if I offer your Abraham the job?"

Winter hugged him. "I knew you'd think of something."

Not long thereafter Alistair sent someone to find Abraham and his family and set them up over the stable.

Chapter 15

That afternoon, Alistair saw a grateful Abraham and his family settled in at the castle house. "Thank Lady Renton, m'lord. God bless and keep you both."

"I'll tell her, Abraham. She'll be relieved to know you are safe."

"I wish there be somethin' I could do for you."

"There is," Alistair said. "Start going to church and give the Lord thanks."

"I'll do that." Abraham pulled at his earlobe. "Lady Renton be a right special lady, m'lord. I owe you, Lord Alistair." Tugging at his other ear, he let out a deep breath as though considering if he should reveal what he knew. "Lord Hollingsworth hates you passionately. This morning yet I went around to beg my job back. I overheard his lordship talking with a foreign-lookin' hawk-faced gent."

Alistair's face gave no hint of his excitement. "Go on, I'm listening."

The groom took a deep breath. "He wants the lady, and he wants to bring you down."

"Did he say how he planned on accomplishing this?"

"No, he saw me then and chased me away."

Putting a hand on the man's shoulder, Alistair told him, "You have done more good than you know with this warning. Thank you."

In front of the little house, Alistair picked up the ribbons. He surveyed the house, recalling without rancor his hopes and dreams when he'd first purchased it for Amelia. It seemed ages ago now. The bitterness was gone. A laconic smile touched his lips. "Thank you, Amelia, for your perfidy in choosing deep pockets instead of love."

Thinking of Winter, he drove away, unaware a blond gentleman saw him driving away and drew his own conclusion he was not loath to share over a bottle of port at Boodle's. Before night fell, half of the beau monde was buzzing with this latest on-dit.

Alistair found Winter ensconced in the library, book in hand. She glanced up as he entered the room. "You did it, didn't you? You rescued Abraham and his family. I've been praying for you."

Accepting her hug, he drew her to him. "A small down payment on my reward," he teased. "He was most grateful to you, my darling. As well he should be." He looked sheepish. "I told him to start going to church and give thanks to God for his rescue."

A tear escaped down Winter's face. "Oh, Justin, you truly have changed!"

With his thumb, Alistair wiped the tear. "I love you." His arm tightened around her protectively as he thought of the groom's warning.

The next morning, Alistair surprised Winter by taking her away from all the wedding preparations. When she came downstairs in her habit, preparing for a ride on Jupiter, she found Alistair waiting impatiently, a secretive smile on his face. Once he had her settled on the restless Jupiter, he swung smoothly onto the roan, which was only slightly less restless than the gelding.

For some time, they rode in companionable silence. Winter kept a tight rein on Jupiter. Reaching Hyde Park, Alistair led the way to a secluded spot under the trees where a repast had been set out on a blanket.

"For you, my dear. A picnic."

Dismounting, they surveyed the collation of delicate chicken sandwiches, fresh fruit, pies and pastries and cheese and lemonade. "You like it?"

"This is a wonderful surprise." Leaning over, she kissed him.

"You are God's wonderful surprise gift to me," he said. Taking her hand he bowed. "Dear Lord, bless this food. And thank You for the gift of Your love. Amen."

His sincerity made Winter again feel she was living some kind of unreal dream, a dream she did not deserve, a dream which could not last. She shook the thought away as they laughed and talked over the delicious meal.

Afterward, they walked among the trees while the retainers took up the remains of the meal. In the shade of a large tree, Alistair pulled Winter into his arms and covered her mouth with his.

A figure saw Alistair's arms wrapped around someone, but could not make out whom the object of affection happened to be. Before discerning the truth of the matter, the person darted from sight with a malicious leer and a tale.

Rumors, growing wilder with each telling, circulated among the ton. More than one unattached female pounced on the on-dit with jealous relish.

* * *

On Sunday Winter and Alistair again attended services at the small church. This time Alistair's eyes glistened as he took in the message. Watching him, peace stole into Winter's heart.

Her peaceful interlude soon ended. When they got home they found Mary waiting for them in the library. "What's wrong, Mary?" At her glance toward Winter, he said, "Go ahead. There is very little she does not already know."

"Terrance has been following Count Abjour. Last night the count made contact with Lord Hollingsworth."

Alistair exchanged a look with Mary. "I thought as much. It is further confirmation. Hollingsworth is our man. Do you think he suspects you?"

"Terrance thinks not. Says the count is frantic to get his hands on a specific piece of information and was pushing Hollingsworth pretty hard."

"Did Hollingsworth indicate he could get the information or do you think the count might try to contact you, as well?"

"You may not like this, but Terrance felt he had to take a chance." Mary bit her lip. "Terrance left word with the count in my name that I knew you had the information he needed. He also said that I feared my cover might be blown and did not think I should be the one to lift the information."

Alistair paced. "What did he have in mind?"

"Thought if we could force Hollingsworth himself to go after the information, we might catch him. If there is another leak, he would know who it was."

Alistair frowned. "I don't like it. I don't want that bounder anywhere near Winter."

"But, Alistair," said Winter, "we have to catch him. Other lives are at stake. Surely I shall be safe enough."

"So you will, if," he said as the idea took form, "we have Aunt Helen invite him to Winter's engagement reception Tuesday evening. It should be quite the crush, being one of the big events of the season. Winter would be well protected in the crowd and the rest of us can keep an eye out for Hollingsworth." He squeezed her hand. "Can you handle that, my dear?"

"Anything so Mary and her husband can be free of their charade."

"That's my tiger," he murmured, and the look he sent her brought a delightful blush to her cheeks.

Addressing Mary, he said, "I'll see the secretary first thing in the morning for some plausible substitute information."

Monday, Winter tried to act as though all was fine, but Winter was anxious about her own reception and the plot to bring down the count and his operation. More was her growing anxiety about her reception in the face of the snatches of conversations quickly aborted when she passed.

"Lord Alistair is a complete hand," she overheard.

"Foolish child."

"Surely she didn't think he would be faithful…."

"Well-endowed, you know."

Doubt about her own worth and Alistair's love for her seeded and grew, however much she tried to stop it. Sleep fled, and Winter buried herself in prayer and in reading the bible, but her prayers were a burden of agony and her reading a blur in the face of her growing suspicions.

Tuesday evening, Mary fastened the last button on Winter's gown. "It is all set," she said. "Terrance and I will be on the lookout for Hollingsworth, and there is nothing for you to worry about. Whatever you do, stay out of the library."

Already jittery, Winter changed the subject. "Did you ever have a reception announcing your marriage?"

"No." Mary sighed. "Terrance was already deep undercover and so was I." She laughed. "Terrance caught me with government papers and dutifully brought me in. You can imagine his chagrin when he discovered the truth of the matter. Terrance was relieved that he and I were working for the same side. You see, we had come to love each other very much."

Patting Winter's hair, Mary carefully added a diamond-studded band made up especially to cover the small bandage still on her head. "We married quietly in the family chapel at Stuart Park, and then came here. Most of the servants are from London and did not know the truth of Terrance's identity."

Winter hugged the other girl. "When this is over, we'll throw a huge party for you and Terrance."

Mary only smiled. She admitted Alistair, whose eyes widened in admiration at Winter's gown of white silk shot with blue and silver threads. She witnessed pride flash in his eyes as he escorted her down to dinner.

Seated at his right, Winter found herself almost too nervous to eat. Later, she had no idea what had been served at the many-course dinner. Laughter and conversation eddied around her. Winter forced herself to smile and speak to the balding peer on her left. Was it just her imagination that more than one glance in her direction held malice, and more than one comment held a double entendre?

Even Alistair's smile seemed forced, and Winter told herself his mind was on Hollingsworth, who sat halfway down the table. She had the impression that Alistair was as relieved as she when the duchess got up, signaling the conclusion of the endless meal.

Winter steeled herself to enter the ballroom. This was all so different from what she had imagined. Though never comfortable with the London round, she had anticipated this reception with joy. Now it seemed more like a nightmare. What if Hollingsworth harmed Alistair or Mary or Terrance? Why did she sense such secret malicious amusement among the guests?

When she entered the ballroom, for a moment she forgot her worries as she breathed in the fragrance of fresh flowers twined around the tall columns with bright streamers and set in exquisite vases in the alcoves around the room.

After Alistair led her out for the first dance, other couples danced while some of the men drifted off to play cards in a nearby room. Older women sat together loudly exchanging the latest on-dits.

Alistair whispered, "Smile. It will be over soon." As she circulated among the guests, Alistair was separated from her.

Though Winter tried to avoid Lord Hollingsworth, he caught up with her. Bowing, he asked, "This dance, Lady Renton."

"I think not, m'lord."

"Do you think you're too good for me now? Let me tell you, your precious fiancé isn't the doting lover you think he is." With that Hollingsworth bowed mockingly.

"I think it is time the two of you to take the floor again," said the duchess, coming up to her. "After all, this is for both of you."

Winter agreed. "I'll get him."

Nearing the group of men laughing and talking to one side, Winter heard snatches of their conversation. Her smile froze, and she moved forward woodenly as all the pitying looks and snippets of conversations coalesced into understanding.

"Well, Lord Alistair, should have known it would not take you long to get back into circulation. You're a virtual inspiration to the rest of us leg-shackled men. Then again, mayhap you and your fiancée might have an understanding."

Alistair frowned. "What are you talking about?"

The dandy chuckled. "Come now, Alistair. You've been seen. Everyone knows you've got a bit o'muslin tucked away."

Glancing up, Alistair met Winter's stricken face. He tried to reach her, but several meandering couples cut them off. Heywood held him back. "She'll get over it, Alistair. After all, you did ask for her hand."

Alistair pulled away. "I don't know who thought up this hen-witted jest, but it is untrue and hurtful."

Heywood tried to soothe his friend. "Have done, Alistair. You were seen at the castle."

"Is that all? I still own the place. If you checked your information you would know a nice older couple rents it."

The dandy spoke up. "That isn't all, Alistair. You were seen in an amorous embrace with a woman in at Hyde Park."

"I don't suppose the individual who spread that on-dit explained Winter and I were having a picnic in a secluded location," he said, barely restraining his fury. "Though I doubt any of you will believe I was with my fiancée. Who started this Banbury tale?"

"Lord Hollingsworth," said the dandy, a flush starting from the neck up at the earl's penetrating scowl. "I tender my apologies for thinking…"

"You should," Alistair retorted. Then, more to himself, he said, "Hollingsworth, that explains it. Hollingsworth!" Glancing around, he could not see the blackguard anywhere. His heart pounded. He couldn't see Winter, either. Pushing through the crowd, he began to search.

Winter stumbled from the ballroom. Dazed at what she'd overheard, Winter clutched her hands together trying to pray a prayer that refused to form. "Help me, Lord. Help!"

Was it all a lie—Justin's profession of faith, his love for her? Was she just a way to free Mary and Terrance and bring down the spy operation? He seemed so sincere. How she wanted to believe him.

The trap for Hollingsworth was forgotten in her pain. She gulped back tears as she slipped into the library, intending to head up to her room as soon as she thought she could do so without being seen. Suddenly she stopped, stilled a gasp.

There was Hollingsworth leaning over the desk, prying it open. If he saw her, she would ruin everything. As quietly as possible, Winter tried to sidle from the room, but lack of sleep had tired her and her leg refused to do her bidding. A less-than-graceful clunk brought forth an oath from Hollingsworth. Over the desk, they stared at each other. "You're stealing the papers," she said when he tucked a paper into his pocket. Her self-chastisement for her slip became a strangled cry, as she hurried for the door ahead of Hollingworth, who reached for her, his expression deadly.

"Let me go!" She opened her mouth to scream, but gagged instead on the linen square Hollingsworth jammed between her teeth. Where were Terrance and Mary? "I laid a false trail. Even now your watchdog thinks he's following me to the stables," he said as though sensing the direction of her thoughts.

Mary, too, would have fallen for the misdirection, thought Winter with despair. *Lord, please let someone see us, please!*

At that moment, Mary came around the corner and stopped at the sight of them. "Hollingsworth, whatever are you doing? Are you planning to jeopardize this whole plan?"

"She found me out, and I can't let her go."

"Let me take care of her," said Mary, holding out her hand.

"No," he growled. "It is time m'lady gets what she deserves. You keep Carlyle and Alistair busy while I have a little uninterrupted session with the chit. Now go!"

Mary backed off. "Don't be long. The count is waiting for that information. He needs it before he can flee the country."

"Don't I know it. I'm going with him. There is little left here for me, but first…"

"Go up to her chambers, third one on the left. I'll see you are undisturbed." Mary's face contorted into a sneer. "About time the little miss has hers. I am tired of being ordered about by the likes of some country miss."

Hollingsworth smiled. "Give me quarter of an hour."

"Done." With a long look toward Winter, Mary pivoted and left her in the hands of Hollingsworth.

Though Winter fought him, he merely picked her up, slung her over his shoulder and sprinted up the stairs to her room. First Justin, then Mary. Winter's heart cried. Was there no one left to come to her aid?

Lord? Helplessness turned to anger. Spitting out the kerchief, she growled, "Traitor."

"Yes, but my own countrymen want to throw me into debtor's prison. The count offered a better deal, even if it did include that insipid daughter of his."

"What are you going to do about me?"

Hollingsworth sneered. "When your body is found, the only evidence will show your lover got rid of you."

"*Body.* Even you wouldn't be so despicable." Her voice cracked. She glanced toward the closed door, praying for some way to stop this nightmare. Somehow she had to keep Hollingsworth from destroying Justin. Mayhap Alistair wasn't all she hoped, but she loved him, and he didn't deserve this. Doubt nagged that she might have misjudged him. Why had she been so ready to believe Hollingsworth and the tittle-tattle of the ton? *Jesus, forgive me if I'm wrong.*

"You won't get away with this." She pulled away.

Grabbing her wrist, Hollingsworth twisted her arm. Step by step he forced her back toward the bed, his devilish expression showing relish at his power over her.

Picking her up, he flung her onto the covers. The bed creaked as he launched himself on top of her, knocking the breath from her lungs.

"Get off of me," she yelled, pummeling him with her fists and kicking as best she could while trying to keep from smelling his breath, foul with alcohol.

Instead he pressed down on her. The look in his eyes panicked her, and she twisted her face away.

"You cannot escape me, Winter. For the last time you have humiliated me."

"You may force yourself on me, but I will never willingly submit," she said through gritted teeth.

"Even if I promise not to tie your demise to Alistair?"

"You're a liar and a traitor and your promises are meaningless," she spat at him. He laughed at her pitiful attempts to fight him.

"You know me too well. Either way, you will be mine." He gripped her hair and tried to kiss her.

Winter clawed at his chest, but he only pressed her deeper into the bed.

Instinctively, she bit him. Roaring in fury, he reared back. Raising up, he slapped her face so hard her head snapped back against the pillow. Again and again he slapped her, his face twisted like some fearsome unreasoning savage.

Thunder exploded in her head and as from a distance she heard herself scream. Ripping the band and patch from her head, he smashed his fist against the side of her head. Dizzily she felt the warm stickiness of her own blood trickle down her cheek.

The sight sent Hollingsworth into a fit of beastly laughter.

Alistair tried to keep his concern for Winter in check as he searched for her—room by room. Stopping a moment, he tried to reason out where she might hide out. In her bedchambers? The library? Mary found him by his rifled desk.

"It's gone. The paper is gone?" he said to Mary as she hurried up to him. "Did Terrance grab him?" Seeing her pale face, he asked, "Terrance wasn't hurt, was he?"

"No, Hollingsworth created a false trail, and Terrance wasn't even here when Hollingsworth lifted the paper, but..." She paused. "Winter was."

"Lord, no!" he groaned. "Where is she now?"

"I sent him on up to her bedchamber to stall for time. He means to have her, Justin. We must hurry."

"I'll get him. You find Terrance," he commanded, tearing out of the library and up the stairs.

Pinning her hands against her waist, Hollingsworth held Winter down. All her screaming and kicking only inflamed him. "Lord Jesus, help me. Send Justin. Justin!"

"Shut up!" Hollingsworth growled, his hand connecting with her bruised face. Again he raised his hand. Winter tensed, waiting, but it never connected.

His face white with rage, Alistair dragged Hollingsworth from Winter and slammed him against the wall, knocking the breath from his lungs.

Before Hollingsworth could suck in a breath, Alistair landed two more punches, leaving Hollingsworth gasping on the floor. Holding him down, Alistair extracted the paper from his pocket.

Hollingsworth quailed under Alistair's cold smile. A moment later the door crashed open, admitting Terrance.

"Help me," Hollingsworth shouted. "This lunatic tried to murder his fiancée and now he is after me."

Alistair handed his brother the paper. "Here, brother, get rid of this traitor before I do kill him."

"Brother!" Hollingsworth slumped. "I…"

"Quiet." Terrance dragged the man to his feet and hauled him from the room.

Furious, Alistair glared down at Winter as she clutched her torn gown. Through wide, frightened eyes, she couldn't help but sense his fury.

Without a word, Alistair found a towel, rinsed it in the water still in the pitcher, sat down on the bed and wiped the blood from her face.

Winter could only look at him miserably, feeling her happiness was as torn and crumpled as her pride and her gown. She looked away, not bearing to look at Alistair's rejection.

He did not want her before, but now, after Hollingsworth's brutal attempt, he could not even pretend tenderness. Closing her eyes, she gave up. She no longer had the pride of running her estate, nor the regard of her fiancé. She had nothing left.

Lord, she cried out silently. *Why?* She stopped, recalling her promise not to ask why, and then changed it to, *What do I do now?*

I am the way. She remembered the verse from childhood. *Trust in the Lord with all your heart...*

As she slipped into unconsciousness, Winter murmured, "Yes. Oh, yes."

Chapter 16

Winter winced as the doctor's fingers probed her reopened wound. Carefully, he rebandaged her throbbing head. Seeing her eyes open, he said, "How do you feel?"

She tried to smile, failed. "Dreadful."

He smiled at that and turned to address his remarks to the earl. "She will recover with time and lots of bed rest for the next week." His frown was stern. "This could have been far more serious."

"I know." Alistair flinched as he glanced toward Winter. "Thank you, Doctor. I'll see to it."

Hungry for a look at Alistair, Winter turned her head only to find the doctor blocking her way. Pouring a nasty-looking liquid into a glass, he held it for her. "Drink it all down, Lady Renton."

She winced. The doctor seemed to assume her expression emanated from the taste and chuckled. "I know it tastes awful, but it will help you rest." Picking up his bag, and with a nod to the earl, he left the bedchamber.

A strange warmth spread through Winter, making her drowsy. "Laudanum," Alistair confirmed, leaning over the bed. His hand gently touched her cheek.

She so wanted to say something. His face swam before her. As he turned away, Winter croaked, "Please don't leave me."

Sitting down, Alistair took her hand. "I am right here, Winter. Right here." The words echoed in her mind as her eyes closed once more.

For a long time, he sat beside her. "Lord," he began, "I don't know how to go about repairing this relationship...but I love her." He continued to pray until sleep finally claimed him, as well.

Early the next morning Mary tiptoed into the room and shook his shoulder gently. "Justin."

Yawning, he opened his eyes. "Mary."

"The secretary and Terrance are downstairs in the library waiting for you. Don't worry, I'll stay with her."

Much to the dismay of his valet, Alistair dressed without his assistance and hurried down to the library.

The sun was already high in the sky when Winter awoke. Alistair was gone and Mary, her head over a book, sat in a chair beside the bed.

Winter tried to stop the tears gathering in her eyes until her chest ached from her effort. Finally a sob broke forth, and her agony burst forth in a flood of tears and hurt and pain.

Throwing down the book, Mary stood up. "Winter, what is it?"

Unable to speak for the tears, Winter shook her head. Still the tears fell.

Just then Alistair strode into the room. Seeing Winter's tears and hearing her wrenching sobs, he waved Mary from the room.

Sitting down on the bed, he enfolded her in his arms. "I'm sorry, Justin. S-sorry."

"What's this?" He winced at the bruises on her face, and from the look in her eyes knew Winter misinterpreted his response.

"Winter, listen to me, you don't understand."

"I heard," she whispered brokenly. "I heard…"

"You heard a lot of nonsense started by Hollingsworth, who saw me coming from the castle and assumed I had installed a lady friend. My dear, we were also seen in the park."

Winter's eyes widened with the horror of understanding. "Oh, no, Justin. I've misjudged you so."

"Shh. It's all right." Looking down at her damp cheeks, he wanted to cry, too. "My darling, I never realized my former indiscretions would hurt you. I am the one who is sorry. I am sorry I didn't wait for you. Sorry I lived the way I did to bring dishonor on myself and to you. I am sorry I put aside my childhood commitment because it wasn't convenient with the way I was living."

"I am not whole. And now, my face."

"Winter, I love you. You've given me back my ideals, my life, my faith."

Searching his face for the truth, she said, "I thought I had lost you. Hollingsworth—" she gulped "—was going to…to… rape and kill me and see that you were blamed."

A hard line formed on Alistair's lips. "He'll never harm you again. He'll go on trial and will probably hang for his crimes. The count managed to evade capture and has left the country with his family. Hollingsworth tried to save himself by listing the men in the government who passed him information. It won't help him, but it did help us round up this operation."

Winter closed her eyes. Alistair almost felt her draw on his strength. A moment later, she drew away. "Mary? Is she really on our side?"

"Yes, she found me as quick as possible. If she had not suggested Hollingsworth bring you to your room, who knows where he might have dragged you. At least I knew where to go."

"Are they free now?"

"Mary and Terrance? Yes, they will slowly reenter society, as heroes."

"Where will they live?"

"I'll have to think on that."

"Someone needs to keep up Renton Hall, and Mrs. Duncan and Mary certainly got along."

Alistair held her close. "Would you mind dreadfully?"

"No, not as long as I have you," she said, ducking her head as red stained her cheeks.

"You'll always have me. One day we'll have a daughter as lovely as her mother and a son to carry on for us both." He swallowed. "Don't ever forget, dearest love. No matter what, I love you."

Putting her arms around his neck, she kissed him, her eyes bright with love.

"'Tiger, Tiger, burning bright....'" he quoted softly.

The shadow of doubt was gone from Winter's face. Snuggling in his arms she interrupted, "I'll live with you and be your love."

"And together we will serve Him."

"Together," agreed Winter, "my one and only love."

Alistair chuckled as his lips found hers in a promise of a lifetime of love and fulfillment.

* * * * *

HEARTSONG

PRESENTS

Look out for 4 new
Heartsong Presents books next month!

**Every month 4 inspiring faith-filled
romances will be available in stores.**

These contemporary and historical Christian
romances emphasize God's role in every
relationship and reinforce the importance of
faith, hope and love.

REQUEST YOUR FREE BOOKS!

2 FREE CHRISTIAN NOVELS
PLUS 2
FREE
MYSTERY GIFTS

HEARTSONG

PRESENTS

HSPDIR13R

LARGER-PRINT BOOKS!

**GET 2 FREE
LARGER-PRINT NOVELS
PLUS 2 FREE
MYSTERY GIFTS**

Love Inspired

Larger-print novels are now available...

LILPDIR13R